The Secret of the Deep Woods

Roy MacGregor

M&S

An M&S Paperback Original from
McClelland & Stewart Ltd.
The Canadian Publishers

For Justin and Matthew Francis – who were blessed by growing up in the wild.

The author is grateful to Doug Gibson, who thought up this series, and to Alex Schultz, who pulls it off.

National Library of Canada Cataloguing in Publication

MacGregor, Roy, 1948–
   Secret of the deep woods / Roy MacGregor.

(The Screech Owls series; 17)
ISBN 0-7710-5646-X

   I. Title. II. Series:

PS8575.G84S43 2003   jC813'.54   C2003-901622-6
PZ7

Published simultaneously in the United States of America by McClelland & Stewart Ltd., P.O. Box 1030, Plattsburgh, New York 12901

Library of Congress Control Number: 2002116594

We acknowledge the financial support of the Government of Canada through the Book Publishing Industry Development Program and that of the Government of Ontario through the Ontario Media Development Corporation's Ontario Book Initiative. We further acknowledge the support of the Canada Council for the Arts and the Ontario Arts Council for our publishing program.

Cover illustration by Gregory C. Banning
Typeset in Bembo by M&S, Toronto
Printed and bound in Canada

McClelland & Stewart Ltd.
The Canadian Publishers
481 University Ave.
Toronto, Ontario
M5G 2E9
www.mcclelland.com

1 2 3 4 5   07 06 05 04 03

"HE'S GONNA HURL!"

Nish didn't even bother cracking back. For once he was sure he *was* going to hurl – no joke this time, no outrageous stunt intended to break up the team and make him, as usual, the centre of attention.

The only attention Wayne Nishikawa wanted at the moment was medical.

And not just one doctor, but a whole hospital if possible, with specialists around the world linked up by the Internet.

Whatever it took to make these hideous cramps go away!

It felt like a hockey game was going on down there. He could feel skates slicing through his churning gut. It felt, at times, as if a Zamboni were being driven through his intestines.

He touched his swollen stomach. It seemed distended, the skin about to split. Something moved beneath his hand. It felt just like his Aunt Lucy's stomach when she'd been pregnant with his cousin, Sydney. Nish had been asked if he'd like to feel the baby move. *He'd never been so disgusted in his life!* But his mother had forced his shaking, clammy hand onto her sister's big beachball of a belly and . . . yes . . . it had felt just like this.

He couldn't be? Could he?

Nish ran the back of his hand across his brow. It was soaking wet. The sweat was rolling into his eyes and the salt was stinging and making him blink, faster and faster.

What if he was pregnant?

He'd be a freak of nature if he were. They'd have him on *Ripley's Believe It or Not!* He'd be on the front page of those stupid newspapers his mother always flicked through when she was stalled in the grocery checkout line:

PEEWEE HOCKEY PLAYER BENCHED FOR BEING
   PREGNANT!
THIRTEEN-YEAR-OLD BOY HAS BABY!
CANADIAN BOY GIVES BIRTH TO GIANT PUCK!

He couldn't be pregnant, could he? How could it have happened? You couldn't get pregnant from showing up at a nudist beach – *could you?*

Nish knew he was thinking crazy. But his stomach was killing him. He tried to calm himself down. He began breathing slowly, deliberately. He bent over to ease the pain and tried to think it through. What had he eaten?

The Screech Owls were on a canoe trip into

the interior of Ontario's Algonquin Park, a wilderness reserve bigger than the Canadian province of Prince Edward Island, and at the gate he'd been made to hand over his precious food supply – licorice twisters, Double Bubble gum, jujubes, Hot Rods, Cheesies, and Mars, Aero Mint, Sweet Marie, and Crispy Crunch chocolate bars – after the rangers had warned the Owls about the danger of marauding bears.

Black bears had been seen at a number of campgrounds in the park. In one case, a bear had ripped a pack right out of the tree where it had been tied for the night and made off with the campers' food. In another, a big bear had trampled a tent down on a terrified older couple, sending them screaming for the lake while the animal ripped apart their sleeping bags in search of some popcorn they had brought to bed as a late-night snack.

That spelled the end of any hope Nish had of surviving in the wilds on his usual diet of sugar, chocolate, licorice, peanut butter, and more sugar – or, as he preferred to call it, a healthy, balanced diet. "A little dairy in the Hershey bars, fresh fruit in the jujubes, and I even make sure I get my greens – green *licorice*, that is."

Muck and Mr. Dillinger had insisted the kids empty out their candy supplies, and they had begun with Nish's pack, which held little else but junk food. They'd taken all this wonderful, healthy nourishment and thrown it into the animal-proof dumpster at the Lake Opeongo outfitters.

Since then, Nish had eaten nothing but the awful, tasteless, boring dried food packs that Mr. Dillinger had brought along and was cooking up for everyone. And *that* was an important point – in fact, the most important point he'd come up with since he'd been stricken with this terrible pain. Same for the blueberries they'd picked and eaten along the first portage.

If everybody had eaten exactly the same food since they started out on Sunday, and this was late Tuesday night, then he shouldn't be the only one about to hurl. If it were indeed food poisoning, then all the Screech Owls would be affected. Travis Lindsay and Sarah Cuthbertson would be out of their tents, too. And Dmitri Yakushev and Fahd Noorizadeh. And Wilson Kelly and Willie Granger and Jenny Staples and Jeremy Weathers. And Samantha Bennett and Gordie Griffith and Lars Johanssen and Andy Higgins. And Derek Dillinger and Liz Moscovitz and Simon Milliken. And Jesse Highboy and his cousin, Rachel. Mr. Dillinger, the team manager, would be out here hurling. And so, too, would coach Muck Munro, whose idea it had been in the first place to head into the bush during the week between the end of lacrosse season and the opening of the Tamarack rink for the upcoming hockey season.

Nish would rather have passed on the whole stupid trip, thank you very much. When Muck and Mr. Dillinger had talked about the joy of canoeing and the pretty sunsets and the chance of seeing moose and deer in the park, Nish had raised his hand and suggested they rent a *National Geographic* tape and order in pizza and pop while they all sat around Fahd's big-screen TV and watched it.

But now here he was, a hostage to Mr. Dillinger's suggestion that the team would "bond" on such a trip – and it was beginning to look like he mightn't survive long enough to watch even one more television show or eat one more string of green licorice.

His stomach was absolutely killing him.

It couldn't have been the ridiculous trick Lars and Andy tried to pull on him, could it? Andy had smuggled in an empty Glossettes box, and he and Lars had filled it with rabbit droppings; they looked just like real chocolate-covered raisins through the little cellophane window in the box. They'd come up to Nish and tried to get him to hold out his hand to take a share. But he hadn't fallen for it. He was too smart for them. He hadn't touched the rabbit "raisins." So it couldn't have been that. He'd eaten some blueberries, but everyone had been picking and eating blueberries, so it couldn't have been that, either.

There was no further sound from the tent Nish was sharing with Travis, Fahd, and Lars. Whoever had whispered *"He's gonna hurl!"* was now snoring with the rest of them.

How long had he been out here?

Nish straightened up. He felt his brow, dry now and no longer cold to the touch. His stomach wasn't churning and twisting quite as sharply as it had been.

He lifted his beloved Lake Placid T-shirt and ran a hand over his stomach.

No movement. No hideous, slimy, three-headed monster about to burst through his belly button and turn screaming on him with razor-sharp teeth in all three heads.

I need some water, Nish thought.

He had no idea where Mr. Dillinger had put the drinking water. He knew, because he had helped hoist it up, that the food pack was high in a tree, dangling from a thick rope, well out of reach of raccoons and bears, as well as highly talented thirteen-year-old defencemen.

He looked off towards the lake. The wind was down now, and the waves very gently lapping the small beach at the foot of the campsite. The path was easy to make out in the moonlight.

Nish began making his way down to the water, a short, thickset young man in a T-shirt with both sleeves ripped off to show non-existent muscles, and his boxer shorts hanging so far down it was a wonder they didn't fall.

A loon laughed somewhere out on the water. Who could blame it?

Nish bowed gracefully towards the call. "Thank you," he said in a terrible Elvis Presley impersonation. "Thank you very much."

He was about to lean down and scoop up some water when, from somewhere high up behind the trees, he heard a strange sound. Not the sound of an animal or a bird, but of something mechanical. Something sputtering, then silent, then sputtering again. Then complete silence.

He looked above him just in time to see something pass over the pines. It was huge, whatever it was.

There seemed to be flames spurting from it, then the flames stopped, then started again.

It was moving very quickly across the sky. There were red, white, and green lights flashing.

It turned suddenly, almost as if it sensed someone was watching from below. Nish thought it was coming straight at him, coloured lights flashing, transforming the entire black sky over Algonquin Park into a giant pinball machine.

He knew instantly what it was.

His stomach wrenched again, stabbing with new pain.

A UFO!

2

"I BELIEVE . . . I WAS . . . *ABDUCTED.*"

Nish winced at his own words, but they were out of his mouth before he could stop them. He wished he could grab them back and stuff them into whatever black hole of insanity they had popped out of. He wished he had never started! It was like he was giving a talk in front of the class and he was the only one who hadn't noticed he'd just peed his khaki pants, or had something green and slimy hanging from his nose.

The rest of the Owls were trying, but not very hard, to keep straight faces as he explained over breakfast what had happened the night before.

"It was probably a refuelling stop," giggled Sam. "They ran out of gas so they came to *The World's Number-One Source!*"

Fahd was laughing so hard he dumped his plate over, Mr. Dillinger's carefully prepared gourmet dried eggs-and-sausage mix spilling out onto the campsite ground, where it was instantly coated with long, rust-coloured pine needles.

"*They shoulda tried his hockey bag!*" shouted Simon.

"Not likely," added Sarah. "I would think even aliens from outer space have noses." She then turned sharply on Nish, her face twisted in mock seriousness. "Or *do* they, Nish? After all, you're the one who spent the night with them, aren't you?"

Nish felt his face burning as red as the flashing lights that had fallen out of the sky last night. There was nothing he could do to stop it. He hated when his face burned like this. He'd even gone to Dr. Witherspoon once, claiming he had a "blushing disorder." He asked the doctor for a pill or a vaccination that would put a stop to it, but the doctor had just chuckled, causing Nish to turn as red as the liquid inside the thermometer Dr. Witherspoon insisted on jabbing down his throat.

He was sure he was even redder than that now. They were all laughing at him – Sam especially, who was pleased to get a little revenge for all the jokes Nish had been making about her new fashion statement. Unusual fashion trends were nothing new to Sam – she'd already been through a "combat" phase and a "skateboarder" phase – but now she'd gone "pop star" on her teammates over the summer, showing up for lacrosse practices wearing baggy sweatshirts studded with rhinestones, bluejean cutoffs with red sequins sewn onto them in strange designs, and a vast variety of colourful T-shirts, each with the face of the latest female singing sensation – none of which Nish could stand.

Well, let them laugh. Nish knew, absolutely, to the bottom of his pounding heart, that the spaceship had landed on the beach at the foot of the campsite. He had felt paralyzed as the huge flashing saucer whirred and hissed and then, ever so quietly, settled down softly while the red and white and green lights continued to spin and flash.

He could vividly remember the door opening like a great drawbridge on an old castle. An extraordinarily white light seemed to pour out of the opening and slip down the gangway and stop, spinning so fast in front of Nish that it seemed to him the light itself had taken form.

And such form! Lizard head and snake tongue, shark body and the furious eyes of a hawk. Eight arms each ended in a different appendage that seemed more tool than hand. One "hand" a wrench, one a Phillips screwdriver, one a can opener, one a long knife, one a hypodermic needle, one a pair of scissors, one a digital camera, one a roll of toilet paper.

Toilet paper?

Well, that was how it looked at the time to Nish. He had been frozen solid, immobilized as the creature injected him with some strange fluorescent serum. And then the creature's knife, with a thin laser of brilliant green light beaming from it, had come down straight from the middle of Nish's head and sliced him perfectly in half.

In two separate parts, Wayne Nishikawa had

been taken up into the saucer and laid out on a table like a perfectly split squash. More creatures made of light gathered around the table like kids in a pet store as the two halves of Nish were poked and prodded and examined.

He could see, but he couldn't move. And what he saw next was so bizarre that – even though he had just told the rest of the Owls that a flying saucer had landed at their Algonquin Park campsite and he had been abducted by aliens from outer space – he could not tell them this part.

Now a different coloured beam of light came from the tip of the knife – fluorescent red rather than green – and it was directed into one side of Nish's swollen, distended stomach. When the tip of the light came out, it was carrying something oddly familiar. Something that looked like cloth, with small Toronto Maple Leafs logos all over it.

Nish blinked with the one eye that could see all this happening.

My boxer shorts?

It made no sense, but the knife had found boxer shorts inside Nish's stomach. They *had* to be what was making his stomach swell up like he was pregnant.

But how had he eaten his boxer shorts?

A third beam of light – yellow as the sun – poured over the boxers, and the underwear began to float up over the dissected Nish, tipped on its side, and began to . . . *speak!*

The aliens asked questions and the boxer shorts answered, the buttons undoing to turn the opening into a mouth!

They asked questions and the boxer shorts told every secret Nish had ever held. Lies he had told, things he had broken, friends he had fooled, tests he had cheated on, even the truth about who had let go the silent sneaker that had all but cleared the gymnasium during the Lord Stanley Elementary School talent show back in June.

"Who does he have a crush on?" the lead alien asked.

"Samantha Bennett," the boxer shorts answered.

"NOOOOOOOOOOOOOOOOOOOOOOOOO!!!!" Nish wanted to scream, but it was impossible to scream with only half a mouth. All that came out was a sound similar to the air brakes on Mr. Dillinger's old bus.

How could the boxer shorts think that? He *hated* Sam Bennett, hated her stupid *girl*-ish clothes, hated the way she kept stealing his best yells – *Kawabunga! Eee-Awww-Kee! I'm gonna hurl!* – and acting like they were her own, hated her for thinking she could play defence as well as he could, hated her for being a hockey glory hound when everyone knew that the true hero, the heart and soul of the Screech Owls, was Wayne Nishikawa.

"Who is the team's best player?" the alien asked.

"Probably Sarah Cuthbertson," the shorts answered. "She's the best skater, anyway. Dmitri Yakushev is fastest, Travis Lindsay might be the smartest. Travis is also team captain, so he might be the most valuable. Sam Bennett's likely the top defence player . . ."

"WWWWHHHHHHAAAAATTTTTTT?????" Nish wanted to scream, but he couldn't.

Why were his boxer shorts lying? What were they trying to do to him? Sarah was good, but who would you want on the ice in the dying seconds of a championship game? And what good was speed when you couldn't finish? And Travis the smartest? Give me a break! Sam the best D? Not in this life!

It suddenly occurred to Nish that the shorts were talking this way for a reason. The boxers weren't lying. They were stating the obvious, and somehow Nish had missed it.

He was dead.

That could be the only possible answer. He was dead, and the boxer shorts were talking about a team that didn't include him. Sarah was the best, now that Nish was gone. Sam was the best on defence, now that Nish could no longer play.

And Travis was smarter — now that Nish had only half a brain.

3

TRAVIS LINDSAY HAD NEVER SEEN NISH THIS BAD.

He had seen his lifelong friend so wound up he could barely talk. He had seen Nish so angry steam seemed to be coming out of both ears. He'd seen Nish in tears, sobbing and bawling like an infant who had just dropped his soother.

But he had never seen him quite like this. Nish looked flustered and frustrated – but he also looked frightened. Terribly frightened.

Travis had no idea what had really happened to Nish during the night, but whatever it was – a nightmare, probably – it had scared him so badly he was shaking as he tried to convince everyone that he'd been abducted by aliens from outer space.

As if, Travis thought, fighting back an urge to burst out laughing in his best friend's face.

One thing Travis did know, however, was that not even a lacrosse ball could bounce about as wildly as Wayne Nishikawa's imagination.

Only Nish could convince himself that aliens had just happened to drop down here in the middle of Algonquin Park, pick Wayne Nishikawa out of an entire campsite of peewee hockey players, and transport him up into their spaceship while they examined him.

Travis laughed to himself. A perfect Nish story! He himself had slept like a baby. He had lain in the tent he'd been sharing with Nish and Lars and Jesse and had listened long into the night to the sounds of the deep forest – the loons calling out on the water, the owl in the trees behind the camp – and once during the night he'd woken up to a light drumming on the tent, rain, only to fall back asleep immediately.

There were beads of water on the tents in the morning, and the sparse grass was wet and cold against bare legs as the Screech Owls moved about the campsite. But the sun was already up, the sky clear and blue, and the water so calm and inviting that Travis figured he had the perfect opportunity to get the camping trip back on track after Nish's ridiculous claim that he'd been abducted.

"*Who's up for a swim?*" Travis shouted.

"*Everybody!*" Sam called back, charging towards the makeshift clothesline, where the Owls' bathing suits had been set out to dry last night.

"*Last one in is an alien!*" yelled Lars.

They grabbed their suits and flew into their various tents to change. They were in and out so quickly it seemed the tent flaps had barely closed when they were tumbling back out, shouting and yelling and heading for the water.

All except Nish.

"What's with you?" Travis asked his best friend.

Nish just shook his head. He seemed near tears.

Travis stared in disbelief. Who always had to be first? Nish, of course. Who always had to be the centre of attention, the star of every moment in the Screech Owls' world? Nish.

And now here he was, sulking like a little child who has just had his hands slapped.

"Get over it! You had a nightmare, that's all," Travis said. "C'mon – we'll dunk the girls!"

That seemed to change Nish's mind. He wandered off to the clothesline, flipped off his bathing trunks, and headed for their tent. Travis set off down towards the beach to join the others.

They were just wading out into the water when they froze at a sound coming from back at the campsite.

"AAAAEEEEEEEEYYYYYYYY!!!"

The blood-curdling scream had come from Nish's tent.

Travis looked at Sarah, Sarah at Travis.

Nish screamed again and came flying out of the tent. He had his bathing suit on, drooping dangerously, and he was holding his back.

"YOU THOUGHT I WAS LYING!" he screamed accusingly at the rest of the Owls. His face was as red as the paint on Muck's canoe.

"*It was so aliens!*" he shouted, his face seemingly on the verge of bursting. "*I found where they put the transistor in me!*"

Nish was turning his back to them even as he walked towards the rest of the players. He was pointing to something near his waistband.

"*They inserted a special device in me so they could control me! Now do you believe me?!*"

Mr. Dillinger dropped his Frisbee and went towards Nish, who was still pointing to the spot. It appeared red and swollen.

Travis looked again at Sarah. She was blinking, her hand up to her mouth.

What had Nish found?

Mr. Dillinger examined the spot carefully. He looked at it from several angles. He rubbed his hand lightly over it. He stepped back, thinking.

"*Well?*" Nish said, unable to keep the self-satisfaction out of his voice. "*Was I right?*"

"It's not a transistor," Mr. Dillinger said.

Nish laughed dismissively. "Well, what is it, then?"

"You really want to know?" Mr. Dillinger said.

"Shoot," said Nish.

"*It's a horsefly bite.*"

4

TRAVIS WAS LAUGHING SO HARD AT NISH'S "transistor" horsefly bite that he hadn't noticed Fahd come down to the beach. He had changed into his bathing suit but his shirt was still on, the buttons open and flapping in the wind.

Fahd was carrying his ever-present Walkman and had the earphones in. His habit had grown even worse over the past summer: if he wasn't bopping to the latest song he and Data had downloaded on their computers, he was plugged in to the all-sports talk station, listening for the latest trade rumours. All the way up to Algonquin Park, he'd sat at the back of the old Screech Owls bus, all by himself, listening for word on who would be the new goaltender for the Toronto Maple Leafs, his favourite NHL team.

But Fahd didn't look like he had just learned the name of the latest player to sign with the Leafs. Nor did he look like he sometimes did when he was playing one of those songs you just *had* to hear.

He looked frightened.

He yanked out the earphones as if they had turned red-hot, then shouted to no one in particular, "*Jake Tyson is missing!*"

Travis could not believe what he was hearing. *Jake Tyson?* The hero of last spring's Stanley Cup final, who had scored the winning goal in overtime in the seventh game? The first rookie to win the Conn Smythe Trophy as the most valuable player of the playoffs since Patrick Roy did it with the Montreal Canadiens way back in 1986? *Missing?*

Impossible. Travis felt like he'd just seen Jake Tyson. And in a way, he had. The NHL star was on the front of the cereal box Travis had opened for breakfast before leaving Tamarack to go on the canoe trip. He'd also been on the front page of *The Hockey News* the mailman had delivered while Travis and his mother were digging around in the garage for his fishing gear. Jake Tyson, the golden-haired, smiling superstar of the Stanley Cup, the greatest Canadian player, they were saying, since Wayne Gretzky.

Fahd was holding out his earphones for Travis to listen for himself, but there was no point – Fahd was already doing an excellent job of broadcasting the news.

"He left three days ago on a fishing trip! They hadn't heard from him, and then sometime last night they picked up a mayday call from the plane he was in! They're saying they think the plane went down somewhere in Algonquin Park – *right here!*"

"*Gimme that!*" Nish roared, snatching the Walkman out of Fahd's hands and clumsily poking the earphones into his still burning-red ears.

Travis knew what Jake Tyson meant to Nish. Nish had claimed the young star for his own right from day one, claiming he'd "scouted" him when Tyson played a season of junior hockey for the Barrie Colts, an hour and a half down Highway 11 from Tamarack. Nish had gone to several of the Colts' games with Travis and Mr. Lindsay, and once, when the young Colts star was leaving the ice at the end of a game, he made eye contact with Nish and flipped him his game stick – a perfectly good Sherwood 9050, which Nish now had hanging in his bedroom.

The Frisbee hockey game was instantly forgotten. The Owls, Mr. Dillinger, and Muck all gathered around the smoking firepit and talked about what Fahd had heard, with Nish – still wearing the earphones – jumping in every now and then to report new details.

"*They say there are rescue planes out already!*" Nish shouted at one point.

The all-sports talk station – which came in badly, the signal fading in and out, the sound crackling and breaking at times – claimed that the Ontario Provincial Police were now trying to pinpoint the emergency locator of the small plane. All planes, from airliners to small float planes, carried a device called a black box, which, the moment the plane went down, would send out signals that could be used to pinpoint the area in which the plane had gone missing.

But so far, the search-and-rescue people had heard nothing.

Jake Tyson had not been alone. The plane was owned, and flown, by a friend of his from Barrie, a man who had been one of the owners of the Colts and had maintained his friendship with the young hockey player. The man, Paul LeSage, was apparently an experienced pilot, with armed-forces training behind him, and the float plane was said to be in excellent condition.

Nish was repeating more of what he had heard when suddenly Muck turned back towards the hills and cocked his ear. He held up his hand for everyone to be quiet.

No one moved.

At first, Travis could hear nothing, then he detected what sounded like a very faint buzzing.

The buzz grew louder. The Screech Owls stood like statues, waiting.

The buzz became a roar, the roar now coming from almost right above them.

Travis looked high into the sky – clear blue now, not a cloud to be seen – but he could see nothing.

The roar became, for an instant, almost deafening, and suddenly it seemed as if two huge yellow birds had burst from the top of the pines and sent huge, startling shadows over the campground as they headed out over the lake towards the far hills.

Then, just as quickly, the planes and the deafening sound were gone.

"Ministry planes," announced Muck. "Twin Otters."

"They'll be looking for the downed plane," said Mr. Dillinger.

"*You mean it happened here?*" shouted Simon Milliken.

"*Jake Tyson crashed here?*" said Jenny Staples.

"They'll be doing grid runs," said Muck. "They'll work their way back and forth across the park until they pick up the signal from the black box. But they must have some reason to think the plane could have come down around here."

"Wasn't around here," offered Mr. Dillinger.

"How do we know?" asked Derek, his son.

"We would have heard it," said Mr. Dillinger, nodding his head up and down decisively.

"Not necessarily," said Muck. "Not if the engine quit on them. It could have glided some distance and nobody would have heard a thing. All they might have seen were the plane's lights."

The words were barely out of Muck's mouth when everyone came to a stop.

The Owls turned as one to stare at Nish, who

still had the earphones in and was frantically trying to tune in to a clearer signal.

He noticed them staring.

He yanked out the earphones, his face reddening. "*What?*"

Sarah was first to speak. "Those lights you saw last night . . ."

"Yeah, I know, you don't believe me," Nish said, twisting his red face in spite.

"It wasn't a UFO you saw," Sarah said. "*It was Jake Tyson's plane going down!*"

Nish just stood there, blinking.

"The *lights*," Sam repeated. "That was Jake's plane, you idiot!"

Nish slowly nodded, realization setting in. The blood was rising in his cheeks.

Mr. Dillinger stepped forward. "Where was it, Nish?"

Nish stared up into the sky, then pointed into the high pines directly behind the campground. "I heard it there," he said. "Just a kind of cough."

"Like an engine that wouldn't start?" Mr. Dillinger asked.

"Yeah, like that. I looked up and saw the lights. But that's all I remember."

"Which direction was it heading?" Muck asked.

Nish thought for a moment, then raised his arm and drew a finger from the trees out over the lake. "That way . . . I think."

Mr. Dillinger shook his head. "That leaves an area of more than a thousand square miles."

"I . . . I didn't see it crash," sputtered Nish. "I thought it landed right here. I guess I must have dreamed that part . . ."

"Dreamed up the horsefly bite, too!" laughed Gordie.

Muck looked once, sharply, at Gordie, who immediately fell silent.

"This is serious business," said Muck. "I think we better fan out and see if we can find anything."

"I'll head up the river," said Mr. Dillinger. "I'll take Sarah's group and Wilson's with me."

Muck nodded. "I'll take Andy's and check the south bay area. Travis, you think your gang could cover the far shore?"

Travis nodded, pleased to be asked. "Sure," he said.

"I don't want anyone getting lost," Muck said in his no-nonsense tone. "You stick together, you wear your safety vests, and you always stay within sight of the water – understand?"

"Yes, sir," said Travis.

5

THEY SPLIT INTO THE THREE GROUPS AND SET out. Mr. Dillinger took two canoes, Sarah in charge of the second, and headed up the twisting Crow River, looking for signs of the crash. Muck took two canoes, Andy paddling stern in the second, and headed across to the south bay to look around. And Travis took charge of the two canoes that remained, Nish and Fahd travelling with him, and Jesse, Rachel, and Simon in the other.

No one knew exactly what to look for. Smoke, perhaps. Or trees clipped by the plane. But all the downed plane had to do was clear the trees nearest shore, perhaps even the far hills, and they would have no hope of finding it. Still, as Muck said, they had to look. Just in case.

They still hadn't eaten any breakfast, but Travis had no appetite anyway. He was sickened by the thought of Jake Tyson being in that plane and knowing he was in trouble. He wondered how helpless the hockey star had felt. He wondered if Jake expected to die or survive. He wondered if Jake *had* died or survived.

The lake was like glass this early in the morning. There were still wisps of fog on the water and it snaked ahead of them as the canoes cut through. At one point, they scared up a huge bird. It took off from a log with a hideous croak, its wings sighing in the silent air as it passed over the two canoes and beyond the trees.

"Great blue heron," announced Jesse.

It all seemed so incredibly peaceful. Travis could hear songbirds in the trees, watched as one small blue bird with a huge head dipped from branch to branch along the shore as if it were stringing Christmas lights.

"Kingfisher," said Jesse.

The tranquillity disturbed Travis. What if the plane had gone down here near the rocks? What if Jake Tyson, NHL star, had drowned right at this point? What if the plane had crashed into the trees and Jake Tyson and the pilot had been burned alive, screaming as they fought to free themselves from their seatbelts? What if the plane had gone gently into the trees and not burst into flame and they were unconscious, strapped into their seats and still alive?

Travis tried to calm himself down, but he couldn't. He watched Nish paddling up ahead, barely bothering to exert himself – "lily pad dipping," Sarah had called it – and wondered if Nish's imagination was also running away with him.

How could it run away any more than it had last night?

Aliens from outer space! Abducted into a flying saucer! Implanted with a special transmitter that turned out to be a horsefly bite!

"What are you thinking about?" Travis asked at one point.

"Huh?" Nish had asked, half turning and nearly tipping the canoe.

"What's going through your head right now?" Travis asked.

"I was just wondering . . . ," Nish began.

"What?"

"I don't know . . ."

"No, tell me."

"I was just wondering . . ."

"What?"

". . . whether fish fart."

Travis stared straight at the back of the thick neck of his thick friend. He could see Nish's colour rising. "I keep seeing these bubbles coming up," Nish went on. "Like when I'm in the bathtub, you know – and I was wondering if fish or turtles fart, that's all."

"You're sick!"

"Well, you asked."

6

THE OWLS WERE STARVING BY THE TIME THEY returned to the campsite on Big Crow Lake. As they drew near they could smell smoke, and it carried the hint of something delicious. Mr. Dillinger was back and cooking up a late lunch. In the distance, Travis could see Muck's party also paddling back towards the campsite. He knew, without even asking, that there was no news.

"Not a sign of anything," Muck said as he hauled his old red canoe up onto the beach.

"None of us saw anything, either," Mr. Dillinger called from the firepit area, where he was whipping up some sort of pasta dish in a large tin bowl.

"What do you think happened?" Sarah asked.

Muck shook his head. "We're only presuming the plane passed over us. Nish saw something all right. A plane, I would guess – but maybe not *that* plane. And even if it was, who's to say it didn't go on for miles beyond?"

"I *saw* the plane," Nish argued. "It was in trouble."

"I thought it was a flying saucer," sneered Sam, "and it was *you* that was in trouble."

Nish said nothing. None of his usual cracks about her outfits. Not even a stuck-out tongue.

Travis knew his friend was too upset to act like the normal Nish – if, in fact, there was such a thing as a *normal* Nish. He had been ridiculed for his story about the alien abduction, and now he had to deal with the fact that his new NHL hero was missing, perhaps dead in a plane crash. Not even "perhaps." *Probably*.

They ate in relative silence for a peewee team that had, essentially, grown up together. The Owls were, by now, almost a family: the players got along, or did not get along, much as brothers and sisters, with Muck and Mr. Dillinger each a sort of extra parent to every youngster on the team. Silence wasn't usual for the Owls, particularly when they were out on an adventure. But silence seemed appropriate, under the circumstances.

Mr. Dillinger was pouring out hot chocolate when the quiet of the campsite was broken by a strange, distant drone from well beyond the tops of the high pines.

"Another plane," said Fahd, pointing out the obvious as usual.

They laid down their cups and hurried out onto the point in order to see.

Seemingly out of nowhere, a large yellow bush plane broke with a roar over the treetops, banked steeply, and went out over the lake, turning and slowly descending.

"*It's coming in!*" shouted Fahd.

The plane seemed to pause in mid-air as it neared the water, then touched down lightly, skipped up, touched down again with a large spray, then settled on the lake, a high rooster tail of water pluming from each pontoon.

"He's carrying canoes," Mr. Dillinger said.

Travis could see two dark-green canoes lashed to the pontoons. What a wonderful way to travel, he thought. Flying into lakes, then having the canoes to explore the shoreline. But then it struck him that these rangers were not here to explore; they had come to find Jake Tyson's plane.

The yellow Otter taxied up to the beach, the doors opened, and two young rangers jumped out into the water, the splash spreading black up the legs of their green work pants.

The pilot cut the engine, and the absence of sound was almost as startling as the roar had been when the plane first passed over the treetops. The engine died with a wheeze, the propeller slowed, and the two rangers muscled the plane in closer to the beach area, where it settled, soft and safe, on the fine sand just as the propeller came to a complete stop.

The front doors opened, and two more rangers, older men, one grey-haired, one completely bald, used the wing struts to swing down onto the pontoons.

The young rangers unlashed the two canoes, turned them over, dropped them down into the water, and pushed them towards the sand.

"Pitch in," Muck said.

The Owls flew down into the water, helping the rangers haul the canoes up onto the sand and then forming a human chain to help load the canoes with the supplies the rangers were pulling from a rear cargo door: paddles, life preservers, tents, ropes, a radio pack, a stretcher, food barrels, rain gear, and cooking utensils.

The older rangers jumped off the end of the pontoons, splashed lightly in the shallow water, and then hiked up the sand and the small ridge in front of the camping area to talk with Muck and Mr. Dillinger. The four men moved back to the firepit area, where Mr. Dillinger had coffee brewing over the fire.

Travis looked at the two younger rangers. They seemed so big and fit, almost like hockey players – one had dark, curling hair that splashed over his collar, the other was blond, or likely blond, as he had shaved his head bald and was tanned darker than the ranger's uniform he was wearing.

"You kids with a summer camp?" the dark one asked.

"We're a hockey team," Fahd told him.

"A *hockey* team?" The ranger burst out laughing. "This lake won't freeze over till Christmas. You plan to wait here that long?"

"We're here for the week," said Sam. "And we don't play on lakes. We play in the Tamarack rink."

"Ohhhh, a little sensitive, are we?" kidded the dark-haired ranger.

Nish couldn't resist. "Ask her about her sissy camping clothes. You'd think she's a *figure skater*, not a hockey player!"

The rangers looked at each other, making faces. "I'm not touching that one," said the dark ranger.

"Me neither," laughed the blond one. "You kids know who Jake Tyson is?"

"We know," said Fahd. "We heard about it on my radio. Nish here saw the plane go down."

Both rangers stopped what they were doing and turned to Nish, who was stepping forward to brag.

"Yeah, I saw it," said Nish, beginning to blush.

"He said it was a flying saucer," said Sam.

"Put a cork in it, fancy pants!" Nish snapped. "I saw a plane go over last night – lights on, but no engine. It was coughing and choking and then nothing."

The rangers looked at each other, suddenly very curious. "Where did it go?"

"He doesn't know," said Sam.

Nish ignored her. "That way," he said, pointing vaguely across the lake.

The rangers looked out. "Towards the river?" the dark one asked.

"We searched the river," said Sarah. "Nothing we could see. We also checked the bay and the far shore. Nothing there, either."

"What do you know about it?" Travis asked the rangers.

The blond one looked hard at Travis, then shook his head. "Probably not even as much as you. The plane's missing. That's about all we know. The air base at Trenton thought they picked up the emergency signal and placed it somewhere around Big Crow Lake, but then the signal went dead. They're still flying search-and-rescue – you probably saw some planes go over."

"We saw them," said Fahd.

"We're here for a preliminary ground search," said the dark ranger. "If they pick up the signal again at the air base, they can radio us and we should be able to get to them."

"Do you think they're alive?" asked Fahd.

The rangers looked at each other as if trying to decide whether to say what they truly felt.

"We don't know," said the dark ranger.

"We can only hope," said the blond ranger.

7

THE TWO YOUNG RANGERS WERE DICK CHANCEY, the blond one, and André Girard, with the curly dark hair. The two senior rangers were Tom McCormick, the grey-haired one, and Jerry Kennedy, the bald one, and they spent considerable time out on the point with Nish, going over and over and over again the events of the previous night as best as Nish could recall them.

The rangers were going to take over an area of the large campsite not being used by the Owls. The smaller campsites on the lake were taken up with canoe trippers, this being the busiest time of summer for travel into the park interior, and the rangers needed a convenient base to work from as they conducted their searches. Besides, the Owls' campsite was the only one with a good wide beach, which made it the only place on all of Big Crow Lake where a float plane could pull right up to the shore.

But the float plane that had brought the rangers was already gone. The canoes and supplies had barely been unloaded when the pilot announced he was heading back to the base. The rangers pushed him off, and the pilot started up the engine, taxied out past the island, and turned into the light wind. The plane roared loudly and moved down the lake in a longer and longer spray until, magically, the spray vanished, the plane lifted, and, in an instant, was gone over the trees in the direction from which it had come.

Travis, Jesse, and Rachel had gone out to the far end of the point to watch. Travis liked being with the two Highboys. They knew so much about nature. They could identify every bird and animal, every fish in the water, even most of the bugs. And they knew everything about the float planes, which Rachel kept calling "Cree taxis."

It was wonderful to see Rachel again. Travis had thought of her often since the Owls' trip to Waskaganish, the little Cree village on James Bay where Jesse had come from and where Rachel, Jesse's cousin, still lived and went to school.

The last memory Travis had of leaving Waskaganish after that amazing northern adventure had been the feel of Rachel's mitten as the two new friends had briefly held hands before the Owls had to go.

It was a feeling Travis had never felt before. A feeling that, he could not help but notice, was back again the moment he saw Rachel waving from Jesse's father's truck as the Highboys pulled up to the Tamarack arena for the final lacrosse game of the season.

Rachel had watched the game, and Travis felt her eyes burning into him as if they carried some kind of powerful energy. He scored four goals and set up three others for a seven-point game, the greatest single lacrosse game he had ever played. Sam and Sarah teased him in the dressing room for playing his heart out for Rachel, and while he had yelled at them to shut up, he knew that they were right.

Rachel had lived up to her promise to come to Tamarack to visit. She was there for the two weeks before school, and Muck, when he heard that Jesse would have to skip the canoe trip to be with his cousin, suggested instead that Rachel join them.

So far, the trip had been marvellous. Rachel and Travis had picked up their friendship exactly where they had left it that day the plane took off from James Bay. Travis felt like he could talk to her about anything.

They were staring out after the rising float plane when Travis happened to look down into the water where it was clear, in the shelter of the narrow point. There were three or four large bass near a stump, their black bodies like darting shadows as they moved in and out between the roots.

There were bubbles rising, small bubbles that seemed to come up out of the sand and vanish when they hit the surface. The words were out of Travis's mouth before he could stop them.

"Do fish fart?"

Rachel turned, her eyes narrowing, as if she were looking at one of Nish's aliens, not her good friend from the Screech Owls.

"*What?*"

"Nish," Travis said quickly, feeling his face heat up like a stove element, "Nish wants to know what makes those bubbles. See them?"

Rachel looked out by the submerged stump. Jesse also looked, leaning forward, his brow furrowed.

"I see them," said Jesse. "It's just swamp gas. Leaves rot. Wood rots. You see it all the time."

Rachel smiled. "But don't tell Nish."

"Why not?" asked Travis.

"We might have some fun with him."

8

THE RANGERS TOOK OFF IN THEIR CANOES shortly after setting up camp, Ranger McCormick with young Chancey heading east, Ranger Kennedy with Girard heading west. They would paddle the shoreline, then take to the old lumbering trails around the lake in the hope of seeing some sign of the downed craft.

The Owls continued with their activities, but no one could really concentrate on what they were doing. They swam before heading out on a long hike in the afternoon to see a rare stand of towering white pine while Muck, the history nut, talked about how most of Canada had once been covered by these giants before they'd been wiped out by too much logging.

Normally, Travis would have listened, but he couldn't help thinking instead about the plane and Jake Tyson and what might have happened. They walked back in silence and were just finishing up their evening meal when the two pairs of rangers returned, almost simultaneously, neither party with any more of a clue than they had setting out hours earlier.

"Not a sign anywhere," said Ranger McCormick. "We got quite a way back on the old trails – but nothing."

"I spoke to headquarters on the radio," said Ranger Kennedy. "Nothing there, either. The emergency signal must have died soon after it started up."

They seemed deeply disappointed.

"Kind of reminds you of Bill Barilko, doesn't it?" Ranger McCormick said to Muck.

Muck nodded, his face downcast.

Jesse Highboy spoke up. "I know about him. We come from Waskaganish. It used to be called Rupert House before we got the Cree name back."

"Rupert House was where he was supposed to go fishing," said Ranger Kennedy.

"He *did* go fishing there," Rachel said. "Our grandfather was his guide. He still has a signed picture Bill Barilko left him."

The other Owls were in the dark. Finally Andy Higgins spoke up.

"*Who* is Bill Barilko?"

"Toronto Maple Leafs. Number 5, defence," announced Willie Granger, the team trivia expert. "Nickname, Bashing Bill. Scored the Stanley Cup–winning goal in overtime against the Montreal Canadiens, April 21, 1951. Never played another game in the NHL. His sweater number is retired. It's hanging from the rafters at the Air Canada Centre. I've seen it."

"Pretty good, son," said Ranger McCormick. "But that's only half the story. Bill Barilko and a friend went off fishing that summer and their plane never returned from Rupert House – sorry, kids, what do you call it now?"

"Waskaganish," answered Rachel.

"Whatever," continued the older ranger, not willing to try the Cree word. "Biggest search-and-rescue ever launched in Canadian history."

"They *never* found him?" Fahd asked.

"The Leafs never won another Stanley Cup all the time he was missing," said Ranger McCormick. "Years went by, and people began to think of it as a curse. Some people even said he wasn't missing at all, that they'd flown over the North Pole to the Communists and he was the one who taught the Russians how to play the game. Some said he was wandering the bush as a madman, his brain gone wonky from the crash.

"Ten years went by and they were still looking for him, and the Leafs still hadn't won another Stanley Cup. It was really, really strange. Then, in the spring of 1962, this bush pilot is out on timber-cruising patrol and gets blown way off course and sees an old plane sticking up out of the muskeg.

"They go in to investigate, and it's the old Fairchild 24 Bill Barilko and his pal took off in. Wings sheared off by the trees, plane half buried in the muck and swamp, both of them still strapped into their seats, except now they were just two skeletons, staring straight ahead like they were still flying home.

"And guess what? That same spring the Leafs win the Stanley Cup for the first time since Bill Barilko scored in overtime."

Nish turned to Muck. "That *true*?"

"It's true," said Muck. "I knew a couple of guys on the Leafs team that won in '62 – Tim Horton and Billy Harris – and they thought there was something to it all. They were convinced that Bill Barilko was haunting Maple Leaf Gardens and they wouldn't win again until Bill's body had been found.

"One of the strangest stories in hockey, that one."

"Well," Ranger Kennedy said, hitching his pants as he stood up from the stump he'd been sitting on, "this here crash is all of one day old. We've still got eleven years to go before we're worrying about any ghost, so we'd better get something to eat and figure out what we're going to do next."

The four rangers set to work preparing their evening meal. Muck went out and stood on the edge of the point, staring out over the water, and no one dared go near him.

Travis knew when the Owls' coach wanted to be alone. Muck had been considered unlucky when he broke his leg so badly while playing for the Hamilton Red Wings that he was never able to play junior again. He never felt sorry for himself, though. In fact, right now, Travis was absolutely sure, he'd be out there feeling sorry instead for Bill Barilko and Jake Tyson and thinking about what truly bad luck was.

Muck returned to the campfire after the rangers had eaten, and the older men sat sipping coffee – and, Travis thought, something out of a small silver flask Muck pulled out of the tent he was sharing with Mr. Dillinger.

The night was warm, the moon now out and very low in the sky, and several of the Owls went down and sat along the point, some of them dipping their bare legs into the water, and talked about the day just past and the plane crash and what was going to happen next.

"Mind if we join you?" a voice said out of the dark.

Travis instantly recognized Dick Chancey's voice. André, the other ranger, was standing beside him.

"C'mon out!" Sam hailed.

The two younger rangers came out along the point and sat with the kids, André in a low crouch as he absent-mindedly plucked small flat stones off the shoreline and effortlessly sent them skipping out across the water. Travis wished he could skip stones like that.

The young rangers were talkative. They told the Owls what they did each summer – making new trails, clearing portages, checking for fishing licences, even a couple of bushfires to fight – and it seemed like the second-greatest job in the world. Greatest, of course, would be to play in the National Hockey League. Or, in the case of Sarah and Sam and the other girls, to make the Canadian Women's Olympic hockey team.

"Aren't you ever afraid?" asked Fahd.

"What do you mean?" Dick asked, chuckling.

"I mean, you're out here in the bush all the time. Sometimes alone. Don't you ever get scared of bears and things like that."

André nodded. He had a long blade of grass in his mouth. He pulled it out, and stared at it thoughtfully. "Well," he began slowly, "there *was* one thing that scared me – but it wasn't a bear."

André looked at Dick. It was difficult to say in the dark, but Travis was half convinced he saw Dick shake his head hard once, as if to tell André to stop. But André was already committed.

"You never heard about Slewfoot, then?" he asked.

Several of the Owls said at once: "Slewfoot?"

"Well," he said, "they say there's an old ranger around here who went mad. They say he lost his canoe on the river in the whitewater and smashed into the rocks when he went down the rapids. It destroyed one of his legs, and he always drags it behind him when he walks.

"He also hit his head on the rocks. He had no idea who he was when he came to. No one knows why he didn't drown like the other ranger who was with him, but he didn't. He took off into the bush and they tracked him and searched for him, but they could never find him.

"Every once in a while we get a report about something being in one of the camps. Campers think it's a bear, but it never does any damage like a bear. All they know is that it breaks into their food and takes off into the night. In the morning they find these strange tracks in the dirt like someone's been dragging something."

"His . . . *foot?*" Simon said in a trembling voice.

"Your guess is good as mine," said André. "I've never seen him, just heard the stories . . ."

"*And,*" a very large voice said from close by, "*we've had just about enough stories for one night, haven't we?*"

André Girard turned sharply, almost ducking as the big voice of Ranger McCormick cut through the night air. They had all been so caught up in the story, no one had noticed the older men coming up on the group.

"That story, kids," the older ranger said, "is what we call a bush myth – it simply ain't so, so

44

don't go thinking about it. There was no such accident. There's no such thing as any Slewfoot."

"Sorry, sir," André said. "Just poking a little fun."

"Go poke away at that fire and get it going again. And no more of that talk, understand?"

"Yes, sir."

"And you kids," the old ranger said, "how about a round of hot chocolate before tucking in?"

"YES!" the Owls said at once.

"We've just been telling Mr. Munro and Mr. Dillinger here what we know from the radio. No sighting. No signals. No one's seen anything, apart from this young man here, who may or may not have seen the plane pass over."

"It was a flying saucer," whispered Sam.

"What's that?" asked the old ranger, turning.

"Nothing," said Sam, giggling.

"Any other questions, then?" the older ranger asked before heading back to the campfire and the hot chocolate.

Nish raised his hand.

Travis rolled his eyes. They were hardly in class.

"Yes, son?" the ranger asked.

"Do you happen to know if fish can fart?"

9

"BREAK CAMP!"

The call came from Mr. Dillinger, his make-shift birchbark megaphone raised to his mouth.

Muck had already spoken to the Owls about the necessity of moving on. They still had the Crow River to navigate, and Muck had booked another campsite on the next large lake in the interior, one that would require a portage of more than a mile – a trek that Nish had been whining about ever since Muck and Mr. Dillinger had first laid out the park map and Muck's big, callused forefinger had traced the route they'd be taking.

"Do they have caddies?" Nish had asked.

Mr. Dillinger had looked up, eyes blinking and moustache sputtering: "What do you mean?"

"A caddy," Nish grinned. "You know – someone to carry my bag."

"We're going canoe tripping, not golfing," Mr. Dillinger had said, shaking his head, and turned again to the map and the long route Muck had mapped out.

So far the Owls had done one long portage, carrying canoes and equipment up a steep hill to the next lake, and one shorter one around some dangerous rapids. Travis actually liked the challenge. He loved the way Muck could simply reach down and swing one of the canoes up onto his shoulders – "*Hey, Mr. Canoe Head!*" Nish had screamed out – and still be able to carry the food pack at the same time.

Travis marvelled at how Muck and Mr. Dillinger had organized the trip, how everything was done with such order. Each of the Owls had his or her own backpack, with clothes and sleeping bag and groundsheet. Some carried special supplies – Travis, for example, had a first-aid kit, others had light tents, tarpaulins, compact tools, or fishing equipment – and then there were also larger packs holding the plastic food barrels and Mr. Dillinger's cooking equipment.

It was all arranged so that, if everyone worked together, no one would have to go more than twice over any portage trail.

They broke camp quickly, loaded up the canoes, and set out, the kids staring back at the rangers' tents, which now seemed so lonely standing on the large campsite. The four men had set out in their canoes at first light to resume their search.

"*Good luck!*" Fahd shouted towards the empty tents.

"*Good luck finding them!*" Sarah called.

"*Good luck!*" several of the rest of the Owls called out.

"Good grief!" Nish muttered at Travis. "How's a *tent* gonna find anyone?"

They paddled easily down the river. Muck said he had never seen the water in the Crow so high. There were even stretches of whitewater: sudden narrowings in the river where the water seemed to squeeze and then jump, the rivulets and currents twisting and turning ahead of them as the Owls rode, laughing and screaming, down each quickwater section.

Travis was paddling stern, with Nish in the bow and Fahd sitting low in the packs trying to switch from side to side with his paddle.

Nish had already given up. He was merely letting the current take them along, his paddle on his knees and his head hunched down towards his lap. He was also looking a little green, Travis thought, though it was hard to believe anyone could get seasick on a little river.

Then Travis grinned to himself – *perhaps Nish was turning into an alien!*

They floated easily, at times effortlessly, in the current. For long stretches Travis found himself getting lost in the scenery. They came across an osprey diving for trout. They passed by a bull moose standing shoulder-deep in the river as he dined nonchalantly on a fresh salad of river weed. They startled great blue herons as the huge birds stalked frogs. The herons squawked once in outrage before rising in such a leisurely and effortless way it seemed they were moving in slow motion, the only sound the wind as it sighed through their broad wing feathers.

Up ahead, Muck was signalling them all into shore.

"What's up?" Travis asked.

"I don't know," said Fahd.

"Unnnnnnnnnn . . . ," said Nish. He did not sound well at all.

The canoes all squeezed into a small natural cove formed by a twist in the river and a small pine-needle-covered point with several large Jack pine hanging out over the flowing water. There was a sand bottom and they grounded softly, the kids leaping out as the canoes struck shore and hauling the boats up onto the beach.

A yellow sign was nailed onto a cedar just behind where Mr. Dillinger stood. It had a picture of a canoe being carried: another portage.

Muck waited until they had all settled down.

"This is usually a portage," Muck said, "especially this time of year. The river gets roughest along here – there's a small rapids just up ahead – and if you tried to make it in shallow water you'd smash.

"The water's deep this summer, though. Deep as it usually is in spring, and I've done the run several times at that time of year." Muck stopped, smiled to himself. "And believe me, you go over in April, you feel it!"

The Owls all laughed at the image of Muck tipping in a canoe. It was hard to imagine.

"I think we can chance it," Muck said. "But if anyone wants to take the portage, don't be shy. It's not that long. Maybe half a mile. And we'll all gather at the end and continue on together."

"I'm walkin'," a voice squeaked from behind Travis. He didn't need to turn to know who it was: Nish, the little green man from Tamarack.

"I'll walk with you," Fahd said.

Travis knew how nervous Fahd was in a canoe. He understood. "We'll walk," Travis said.

"We'll come with you," Sarah said, stepping over beside Travis.

"You don't have to," Travis said, but secretly he was pleased.

"Sam and I and Rachel need to stretch our legs anyway," said Sarah.

Travis nodded, worrying that he was blushing. He had hoped it wouldn't just be Sarah. That her whole canoe – Rachel included – would be coming along the portage.

"Anyone else?" Muck asked.

"*Rapids!*" Gordie Griffith shouted out with enthusiasm. Gordie was probably the best canoeist of the Owls, and he'd been hoping for some excitement.

"*Yes! Rapids!*" shouted Simon Milliken, the least likely of the daredevils.

"*Rapids!*" called out Jesse and several other of the Owls.

Muck looked at Mr. Dillinger, who nodded. They seemed to have a plan.

"You six kids will have to take your packs, okay?" said Muck. "Just stick to the trail and there's no problem. Mr. Dillinger and I will come back for your canoes."

"That's hardly fair," said Travis. "You shouldn't have to carry them for us."

Muck grinned and winked. "Who said anything about carrying?"

Travis smiled. Of course. Muck would like nothing better than a chance to run the rapids on his own.

Mr. Dillinger would be another matter; he was red-faced, swallowing hard, and scratching the three-day growth on his neck.

No, Travis wasn't so sure about Mr. Dillinger at all – but Muck would take care of him, that was a certainty.

10

TRAVIS DIDN'T REALLY MIND MISSING THE whitewater. The sun was now high, and it was much cooler in the woods than it had been on the water. The trail was well marked, and he could handle his own pack easily.

Nish was trudging along behind, struggling with his pack as if they had forced him to strap a minivan to his back. Travis could hear his friend grunting and moaning and complaining with every step.

Rachel, even with a large pack, moved with perfect ease through the woods. Travis had noticed it before. It was as if Rachel somehow *fit* the bush. Nish might look like ... *well* ... an alien from outer space out here in the bush, and Travis himself might move well enough, but there was a difference. Travis knew he moved best, not even bothering to think about his steps, whenever he was in a school corridor or on a hockey rink or along any of the streets in Tamarack. In the bush, he sometimes stumbled, sometimes kicked off roots or stones or forgot to duck for branches. Not Rachel. She moved like a fish through water when going along the trail, never a wasted movement, never a wrong move.

Rachel and Travis walked together and were soon deep in conversation. They had been catching up on each other's lives at every opportunity since Rachel had shown up that morning for the bus ride up and into the park, and it seemed to Travis now that he knew more about Rachel than practically anyone else he knew – Nish excepted, of course.

They walked easily together, pausing every so often to make sure Nish was still coming along behind.

"Here – let's pick it up," said Rachel after a while. "Fahd and the girls are well ahead."

They turned and stared down the path. Nish was struggling as if he were carrying the last stone they would use to complete the pyramids. He was soaking with sweat and had attracted a swirl of mosquitoes and horseflies that he kept absent-mindedly swatting at as he dragged himself along.

"C'mon, Nish – hurry up!" Travis called. "We'd better catch up to the rest."

"I've changed my mind," Nish called back. "I want to go by canoe."

"Too late," Rachel shouted. "They've already left."

Nish made a face that could have crushed a walnut, hiked up his big pack and trudged on past them, heading up the trail.

Sam was coming back towards them without her pack. "The trail splits ahead!" she called as she came through the trees.

"Huh?" was all Travis could say.

"It splits, goes two different ways, and we can't tell which is the right one."

"Muck said the path is clearly marked."

"It is clearly marked – it's just that there are two paths. It looks like there might have been a sign to tell you which branch to take, but it's been broken off and we can't find it."

Nish looked worried. "What'll we do?"

"We can all go back and wait for Muck – and waste everyone's day – or we can figure it out," said Sam.

"Let's have a look," said Rachel.

Nish, Travis, Sam, and Rachel picked up their pace and soon reached the spot where Fahd and Sarah were waiting. Fahd was lying on his back with his Walkman out and his earphones in. He had his eyes closed.

"*Any news?*" Nish shouted when he saw Fahd. Fahd didn't hear him.

Sarah shook her head, disappointed. "Nothing good – the radio says this region's in for a bad storm tonight or tomorrow."

"*Great!*" snarled Nish. "Just what we need is more water for Muck's stupid river!"

No one paid him any attention.

Sarah pointed out the two trails, both obvious, each going off in a different direction.

"It's got to be this one," Sarah said.

"That makes sense," Rachel said. "It's the one going back towards the river."

"How can you tell?" demanded Nish.

"How can you *not* tell? We got out on the east side of the river, didn't we? And we've been walking straight east and we haven't crossed over the river or anything. And this trail heads east while that one's going northwest. How can this one not be the right one?"

"Look," Nish snapped. "I didn't come here to do a geography exam – I don't even know *what* I came here for. Just make sure you take the right turn, okay?"

"Now there's a happy camper," shot Sam.

Nish just turned and spat into the dirt: end of discussion.

They set out on the trail Sarah and Rachel had picked out. Travis felt immediately calmed by this unexpected twist. The trail was well travelled, and it seemed to be headed in the right direction.

They passed by a third trail, heading off to the left, but it was narrower and less beaten down. They ignored it.

They climbed a long hill, and then another, and then came to a bluff they had to get around, which they did by picking out a tall tree and heading for it.

They got there all right – but now the trail was gone.

"It's just trickled away," said Sarah. "One minute it was a perfectly good trail, the next minute nothing."

"What'll we do?" whined Nish.

"Go back," said Sam matter-of-factly.

Nish groaned as if he were dying.

"We'll just go back to where the trail first split," said Sarah. "It's obvious. We just took the wrong path."

They headed back, the girls singing an old camp song, Nish still whining and sulking and moaning and complaining with every step. No one paid him the slightest heed. They came back to where the narrower trail headed off, now to the right.

"This is the little trail," remarked Sam.

"*Take it!*" shouted Nish from behind.

"We should go all the way back," said Travis.

"Think about it, dumb one," Nish shouted with scorn. "It's pretty obvious we're not the first to get suckered up this wrong trail. This is the path people have been using to get back onto the right one."

"Makes sense to me," said Sarah.

"Sure would save us time," said Sam.

"We shouldn't," said Travis.

"*You're such an old woman!*" Nish hissed from behind. "Are you going to go through life never taking a chance?"

Nish's words stung. They hurt because, in a terrible way, they were kind of true. Travis didn't like risk. He liked certainty. He liked things you could count on.

"Nish is likely right," said Rachel. "It goes in the right direction. And it would save us close to an hour, I bet."

"I say we go down it a bit, and if it's not working out, then we come back this way and turn . . . right," said Sarah, relieved that she had her bearings.

Nish didn't wait. He started down the trail happily, now whistling like one of the seven dwarfs off to work in the diamond mines.

Travis shrugged. It probably made perfect sense. He was just being, as usual, too cautious, too unwilling to take a chance.

They walked for fifteen minutes, brushing through cedar and low spruce, stepping over fallen logs and walking, at one point, carefully along a boardwalk that someone had thoughtfully laid through a bog.

Travis thought the trail was getting ever thinner.

They crested a hill, then another. They headed down along a creek bed, jumping from stone to stone, and came to where it seemed the trail should pick up again. But there was nothing.

Nothing at all.

"We've lost the trail!" Sam said, a tremble in her voice.

"We go back," Rachel announced immediately.

Back up the creek bed they went, at times splashing into the water, at times slipping on the rocks.

It seemed to Travis they'd been walking along the creek bed longer heading back up than they had going down. He could feel his heart beginning to pound. He worried that Rachel might hear it and think he was afraid.

"Where did we come down onto this?" asked Fahd.

"I think back there," said Sam.

"I don't think we've come to it yet," said Sarah.

Only Nish was willing to state the obvious. "WE'RE LOST!!!"

11

TRAVIS WAS IN SHOCK.

Several times his grandfather had warned him about the dangers of getting lost in the bush around the cottage – "A man can become completely disoriented fifty steps off the trail," he would say – but he had never fully understood how easy it was until it happened.

And there was no doubt in Travis's mind that they were lost.

He stared up into the trees and spun about. No buildings to head for, no highway sound to follow, no path, no sight lines at all except for straight up into the rising boughs of the pines and a hint of the sun as it flickered through the branches. He couldn't even tell which way the sun was moving. He hadn't the foggiest notion whether they were moving north or south or east or west.

Nish was panicking. He was darting, first one way, then the other, in search of the trail. His face was so red it was a wonder the sweat pouring off his face didn't boil.

"The first rule to remember," Travis's grandfather always said, "is *not* to panic. Sit down, get your bearings. And if you're completely lost, *stay put*. Don't waste your energy running in circles."

Travis was about to impart his grandfather's wood lore to the others when he realized Rachel was already far ahead of him. She had removed her pack and was checking the trees, running her hands around the bark of a hardwood.

She stepped back and pointed. "That will be north."

"How can you tell?" Sam asked.

"There's moss on the far side of that beech — moss likes the north side of trees."

"What good does that do us?" Nish moaned, dropping his pack hard, a beaten man. "We're not trying to find the North Pole!"

No one paid him any heed.

Rachel stood for a long time trying to figure out where they were in relation to the river. She seemed to be talking to herself at times, pointing in various directions, mumbling, shaking her head.

"It's impossible without a map," she said finally. "I don't know how the river runs. If it's straight north, which is the direction we were going when we began the portage, then we could head east and know we'd reach it eventually. But who knows what twists a river can take?"

"What do we do, then?" asked Fahd. His voice was trembling. He was clearly afraid.

"Did anyone see the map when Muck and Mr. Dillinger had it out?" Rachel asked.

"No," said Travis.

"No," said Sarah.

"No."

"No."

"I did," Nish announced.

Everyone turned to him.

"I was trying to rifle an extra granola bar," Nish explained, still red-faced. "They were so lost in the map that they didn't even see me."

"Did you see the river route?" Rachel asked.

"Yeah, I guess."

"Which way did it go?"

"How do I know? I can't read maps."

"Could you see where we were headed?" Fahd asked.

"Muck kept tapping on a lake saying he knew of a good campsite on some island."

Rachel got excited. "Where was the lake?"

"On the map," Nish said impatiently.

"No, stupid — where on the map was it? East? North?"

"How should I know?" Nish answered, growing annoyed. Then he brightened. "It was to the *right*!"

Sam groaned. "*That* doesn't help, map boy."

"No, wait!" said Rachel, suddenly excited. "Maybe it does. Where was Muck sitting?"

"I don't know," said Nish, again annoyed. "In front of the map, obviously."

"Where was Mr. Dillinger sitting?" Rachel asked.

"Off to the side. He was fiddling with the fire and kept leaning back to look."

"So," Rachel said, nodding with satisfaction, "we can presume Muck was sitting directly in front of the map, with it facing him. And if the lake we're heading for was directly to the right, as Nish says, then that would have to be east."

"How so?" asked Travis.

"Maps run north–south – if the lake was to Muck's right, it would be east of the river route he was plotting."

"What good does that do us?" asked Sarah. Her voice, too, was trembling slightly.

"Well," said Rachel, "we know where north is. And we know the river and the lake we're heading for is to our east. So at least we won't head north or west and be lost forever."

"You think we should move anywhere?" Travis asked. "My grandfather always said if you get lost, stay put."

Rachel smiled. "Crees don't get lost, Travis."

12

THEY BEGAN WALKING DIRECTLY EAST. RACHEL kept north in check through the tree moss and, every once in a while, they passed through a clearing that allowed them to monitor their direction against the sweep of the sun. It was now late afternoon, and as long as they kept the sun to their back they'd be heading in the direction they wished to go.

It all looked the same to Travis. They pushed through overgrown logging trails and were fooled, twice, by animal runs that the other kids took for human paths, but which Rachel persuaded them were not.

It was rough going. The spruce branches and raspberry canes scratched and tore at their bare legs. Logs and stumps hidden from view knocked their shins and tripped them up. Rocks gave way, weeds entangled, and flies buzzed and got in under baseball caps, driving the kids crazy with their biting.

They had talked and even sung at first, but now no one said a word. The seriousness of the situation was beginning to sink in. A few hours ago, Travis was wondering if they'd make it out before dark. Now he was wondering how they would spend the night, having all but given up hope that they'd suddenly break through into a clearing, with the river and the rest of the Owls waiting patiently for them.

He heard a roar like a giant stomach rumbling. Everyone turned at once, staring back at Nish.

"*Not me!*" he shouted.

"*Who else?*" Sam snapped back sarcastically.

"It's the storm moving in," said Rachel.

The storm. Travis remembered. There was supposed to be a huge storm building up, according to the rangers, and now it was coming in on them.

"What should we do?" asked Sam.

The six kids stopped. Everyone seemed to be waiting for Rachel. It was as if she'd been elected captain, Travis thought. Everyone knew she knew so much more about the bush than any of the rest of them. They'd be crazy not to defer to her on what to do.

"We better face up to it," said Rachel. "We're here for the night."

"I'M GONNA DIE!" Nish wailed.

"Sooner than you think," said Sam, "if you don't shut up."

"We need to look for a place to settle in," Rachel continued. "Higher ground if it's going to pour."

With Rachel leading the way, they began to look for a suitable place to set up camp. Travis instantly gained new appreciation for the groomed campsites they had left behind, with the carpet of soft pine needles, the firepit, smooth places for the tents, and even a rough outdoor toilet.

"Over here!" Fahd called, just out of sight. They raced over to him.

"Looks good," said Rachel.

Fahd had stumbled onto a perfect glade, like a shining green jewel in the sunlight, with the dark woods surrounding it like a wall. There was grass here, and if the ground was not quite flat, it was surely flat enough for them to pitch tents on.

Travis stopped in his tracks.

"Do we even *have* tents?"

"Better check our packs," said Sarah.

"*Ahhhhhhhh* . . . ," Nish began sheepishly.

The other five turned instantly, knowing instinctively something was wrong.

Nish was beet-red. "I don't have my pack," he said, swallowing hard. "I set it down. Back there somewhere."

"How far back?" asked Travis.

"I don't know – back there."

"That could be anywhere," Rachel said. "We'll just have to get by without it. Let's see what we've got here."

They rolled the remaining packs down on the soft ground and began to open them. Travis laid out what he already knew was in his pack. Groundsheet, sleeping bag, clothes, toothpaste and toothbrush, a box of pills in case his allergies hit, water sandals, bathing suit, compact fishing rod, and the first-aid kit he'd been assigned.

He hoped they wouldn't be needing it.

"*Tent!*" Sam shouted. She hauled out the carefully folded tent and tossed it out on the ground. It was one of the smaller ones, suitable for three.

Sarah and Sam got to work putting up the tent. Travis and Fahd worked on finding large rocks to make a firepit.

Nish, who was supposed to be helping Rachel search for firewood, sidled over to Travis. "How come *they* get the tent?" he whispered.

Travis dropped the rock he was carrying. "Huh?"

"How come *they* get the tent?" Nish repeated. "Why *them*?"

"Maybe because it was in *Sam's* pack?" Travis suggested with as much sarcasm as he could muster. "*Ours* was probably in *your* pack!"

Nish shook his head. He was still sweating. "They want equality," he said. "They want to be treated as equals on the team. But then they get here and demand to be treated as *girls*." Nish said the last word as if it were something he'd pulled out of a cat-litter box.

The sky was darkening now, thick clouds the colour of an old bruise rolling in and covering the sun. The wind was also up, the temperature dropping.

"That'll do for the wusses," Sam said as she stepped back from the completed tent. "What're we girls going to do for shelter?"

"There's a tarp in my bag," Rachel said. "We'll string up a lean-to."

Nish was blinking, incredulous. "*We* get the tent?"

"Sure," said Sam. "*We* know who the weaker sex is."

"You can't do that –" Travis started to say, but Nish cut him off.

"Speak for yourself, Tarzan," Nish snapped. "*I'm* in the tent."

Rachel was already at work on the lean-to. First, using a tool that looked like a combination shovel, pick, saw, and small axe, she built a frame: a long cross-pole supported at either end by two shorter poles with Y branches at the tops, which she drove firmly into the ground. She cut two more posts and angled them down to the ground from either end of the cross-pole away from the fire.

Rachel, Sam, and Sarah then tied the large orange tarp down over the frame so that the lean-to took on the appearance of an open-sided tent. They tied down all the lines, and then Rachel went back into the bush, snapped off cedar branches, and piled them over the tarp to keep the plastic down in the wind and give the structure even more substance.

Travis was impressed. In an hour or less, Rachel had built something that would have taken him a week and never been so good. It looked almost *permanent*.

The girls laid out their groundsheets inside and pulled the corners of the tarp down to form a rough doorway, which they could tie down or else leave open facing the fire pit.

"Can I interest you girls in a good tent?" Nish said good-naturedly. He too was impressed.

"We need a fire," said Sam. "Fahd, you said you have matches?"

"Right here."

Rachel was already building a small crib from the wood the girls had collected.

"There's no kindling to start it with," Fahd said, in a bit of alarm. "No newspapers here, either."

"We'll use Cree newspapers," Rachel said, laughing.

She walked back into the bush until she came to a large spruce, then she pushed through its dark skirt of low prickly branches and ducked completely inside.

They could hear her snapping off branches.

In a minute, she came out again, her arms filled with tiny dead branches from low down inside the spruce. "Remember this one, Nish," she said, giggling. "These branches are always dry – even in a storm." She set down a handful of the dry branches on the top of the crib and, with one match, got a magnificent fire going.

It was quite cool now, the wind picking up, the day rapidly darkening under the threatening clouds. The kids drew close to the fire, but less, Travis thought, for warmth than for comfort. There was something incredibly reassuring about the tent, the perfect lean-to, and the fire Rachel had built. He was no longer quite so afraid.

"All we need are some hot dogs to roast," giggled Travis, holding out his hands to enjoy the blaze.

"Or popcorn!" laughed Fahd.

"I'm starved!" Nish said. "I'm gonna die if I don't eat soon!"

"So," said Rachel, "eat, then."

Nish snorted. "Yeah, sure. What am I gonna do? Dial 567-1111 and give Pizza To Go twenty minutes to get here or it's *free*?"

"There's better stuff than pizza out here if you know where to look," Rachel said. "Give us fifteen minutes. You boys keep the fire going and gather up some more wood for tonight."

13

FAHD AND TRAVIS LOST TRACK OF THE TIME AS they built a good-sized store of fuel for the night. There were rumblings of thunder now, and when Travis looked back in the direction from which they'd come – or from which he *thought* they'd come – he saw lightning flash in the clouds. It looked like a bad storm coming.

"Dinner is served!" Rachel's voice rang out.

The girls laid their finds down on one of the groundsheets in the lean-to. They had red raspberries held in a loose sling in Sam's shirt, blueberries in a tied-up kerchief, several varieties of mushroom, puffball, wild leeks, cattails, and a second shirt full of soaking, sopping water lily.

"If we only had a pot or two," said Rachel, "I could cook us up a feast."

"Where's the food?" Nish said, looking over the array of mysterious plants.

"No pizzas, Big Boy," said Sam. "But enough to keep you alive."

They began to eat the raw food. The mushrooms, once cleaned, were edible. Travis liked the cattail roots, but the water lily he could do without. The berries, of course, were absolutely delicious.

"I'll have some of them," said Nish, taking a handful of blueberries, then a second.

"See," said Sarah, "it's not so bad."

"Eat your moose food," Nish snarled. "I'm merely having my daily intake requirement of sugar."

CRRRRRRRRRAAAAAAAAAACK!!!

Everyone jumped. It seemed the sky had suddenly split apart.

"*It's here!*" announced Rachel.

They ducked in under the lean-to, and in an instant the thunder broke. The rain came down like shotgun pellets, hammering the little tent and the lean-to.

The fire fizzled and died, the smoke from the logs twisting away and vanishing.

The kids, however, stayed dry. Perfectly dry.

It was darkening fast.

"Nothing to do but try to sleep," Rachel said.

CRRRRRRRRRAAAAAAAAAACK!!!

The second strike was even closer than the first. Travis shook. He thought he heard wood splintering higher up the hill.

"TRY TO SLEEP?" shouted Nish. "I'M GONNA DIE!!"

CRRRRRRRRRAAAAAAAAAACK!!!

CRRRRRRRRRRRRRRRAAAAAAAAAAACKKKKKK!!!

14

TRAVIS HAD NO IDEA HOW LONG HE HAD SLEPT, but he was suddenly aware of an enormous stillness.

The rain had stopped.

He listened a long time, and only faintly in the distance could he hear the slightest hint of thunder. The storm had passed over.

He had no idea what time it was. He could hear the tinny sound of Fahd's radio. He listened to Fahd's breathing until he was sure he was asleep, then reached over and flicked off the radio to save the batteries. Nish was snoring.

Travis had to go to the bathroom. He struggled out of his sleeping bag, careful not to disturb the other boys, and unzipped the front of the tent.

The clouds had moved on and the sky was clearing now, allowing for some moonlight. Travis stepped out, his bare feet sinking into the soaking ground. It was like stepping through a swamp, the dirt and pine needles and grass squishing up between his toes and each step followed by a sucking sound that seemed to be trying to pull him back.

He moved to the edge of the glade and relieved himself, careful to ensure that the sound didn't wake anyone – especially the girls!

He was standing there, waiting to finish, when Travis was struck with the strangest, eeriest feeling he had ever felt in his life.

Someone was watching!

There were eyes somewhere in the dark, and they were boring into him!

Travis shivered. Not from cold – the air had warmed again with the passing of the storm – but from a terrible sense that something menacing was watching him, and waiting.

He was almost too scared to turn. He considered calling out, but was afraid he'd be ridiculed if it turned out to be nothing.

Slowly, Travis turned around, ready to jump if necessary. He could see the tent, the lean-to, and the firepit. He could see where they'd stashed their packs under an edge of the tarp. He could see where the moonlight petered out and the black apron of the woods began.

He could see eyes!

Never in his life had Travis felt such a chilling tremor go up and down his spine. It felt as if his hair were standing straight on end.

The eyes were yellow, gleaming in the moonlight like miniature headlights – and Travis felt himself frozen.

Suddenly the eyes moved.

The creature moved smoothly, catlike. It loped silently past the firepit. *A wolf!* It was still staring at Travis when it suddenly swept in under the spruce trees and vanished into the darkness.

Travis breathed out. Without realizing it, he hadn't taken a breath since he felt the eyes on the back of his neck. He was shaking, shaking like a leaf, even though it was hot enough for him to be sweating.

His head was spinning. *A wolf? Was it dangerous? Would it attack?* And yet, Travis thought, all it had done was stare at him and then move off. No growl, no snarl, nothing. Just curiosity, and then it was gone.

His heart was pounding. He could hear it in the silence, could feel the blood pumping through his temples. He felt light-headed, almost as if he were about to topple over.

Travis made his way back to the tent. He could hear Nish snoring, could pick out, faintly, the breathing of the sleeping girls. *Should he waken them? Wouldn't he just scare everyone if he told them about the wolf?*

It was gone, he decided. He should try to get some sleep.

Maybe he hadn't even seen it at all.

But Travis could not get back to sleep.

He lay in his sleeping bag trying to get comfortable, trying a dozen different positions, but nothing worked. His body might have been tired, but his mind was racing.

Was Muck trying to find them? Was the wolf still there? What was happening in the search? Was Jake Tyson dead or alive?

Travis shook his head and tried to think of other things – his grandparents' cottage, heading back to school, the upcoming hockey season – but more worrying thoughts kept intruding. He gave in to his fate and simply lay there, waiting for morning to come.

It was so quiet now. Nish wasn't even snoring any more, not since he had shifted abruptly in his sleep, mumbling something about talking boxer shorts.

Travis tried counting sheep. He tried going over every goal he had scored that summer in lacrosse, then every goal he had ever scored in hockey. He tried to remember his top ten favourite tournament games. He tried to remember the names of all the teams the Screech Owls had ever faced . . .

. . . and then he heard the sound.

At first he thought it was his imagination. Or maybe it was the wind picking up. But it was neither. It was a sound unlike anything Travis had ever heard before. A sound like something heavy being pushed or dragged.

And then he heard the breathing.

Heavy breathing.

It was large, whatever it was.

A moose?

A bear?

Travis reached for his shorts and, very quietly, afraid even to breathe, dug around in his pocket until he found his jackknife. He pulled it out and opened the blade, ready to fight back.

He felt like a fool. What good would a little Swiss Army knife do against a bear? One swat and the knife would be flying into the bush. But if he had to fight, he would.

He was ready to jump up. The second he heard the bear trying to get into the tent or the lean-to.

He lay there, shaking, near tears, and listened.

The heavy breathing continued for some time.

And once in a while, the other sound, the sound of something heavy moving.

Then, suddenly, all went silent.

Travis lay, finally able to breathe. He thought he could hear branches snapping some way off in the bush, but soon there was nothing.

Silence.

And then he fell asleep.

15

TRAVIS HAD NEVER BEEN SO HOT.

The tent seemed to glow with sunshine, and the atmosphere inside was warm and stale. He rolled over, yanked on his shorts and T-shirt, and rolled, gratefully, into the freshest, sweetest air he had ever encountered.

He sat there, taking it all in, blinking while his eyes adjusted, and wasn't at first aware that he was not alone.

Rachel was already up. She had their only plastic container – a Tupperware bowl that normally held Sam's soap and toothbrush – and she was smiling.

"I'm going to find us some water," she said. "We'll need to drink, otherwise we'll get dehydrated."

Travis smiled back. "Why didn't you just set it out last night? It would be full by now."

"Good thinking, Trav," she said. "We'll do it tonight if we have to stay another night here."

"We'd better not."

"You never know. I think I know where to find some fresh water. There's a little creek just over to the side of the hill."

"Don't get lost!" Travis called after her as she set out for the water.

Rachel turned, laughing. "You keep forgetting – I'm a Cree. We're never lost."

Travis rose and stretched hard in the sun. He was stiff from sleeping on the ground, but he must have slept enough, for he was no longer tired. The sun was warming, the air so fresh from the storm that it felt energy-charged, and he found he was in an excellent mood despite the fact that they were lost in the wild and had no idea whatsoever where they were.

"You're up," a voice said from the far side of the lean-to. It was Sarah. She was walking around bent over, her hands on her knees as she stared down hard at the ground. "Did you hear anything last night?" she asked.

Travis swallowed. "Like what?" he asked.

"Like a large animal moving around out here," Sarah said. "I was sure something brushed against the lean-to – almost knocked it down – and then I could hear this strange noise."

"Like what?"

"I don't know. I could hear breathing, and it didn't sound good, or else whatever it was was dragging something heavy along. I actually imagined it might be one of you guys."

"I heard it, too," said Travis. "I thought it was a bear."

"Muck said you'd smell a bear. 'Like a skunk, only worse' – remember?"

"Yeah."

"No smell. And no paw prints. No moose tracks, either – I thought it might be that. But come and look at this." Sarah was pointing, outlining a shape in the soggy ground.

Travis stared hard. He couldn't tell what it might be.

"It's a footprint," Sarah said.

She got down on her knees and very carefully traced its outline. The ground was soft and wet, but there could be no mistaking it: a human footprint, a boot.

"Put your foot down on it, Travis."

Travis did as Sarah asked. He very carefully placed his sandalled foot down onto the footprint. "Not my size," he said. "Much too big."

Sarah looked up. "What about the other boys?"

"Nish and I are about the same. Both of us are bigger than Fahd."

"And it's not one of us, either," said Sarah, placing her sandal into the large print. "Sam's slightly bigger than I am, but not nearly as big as this."

Travis couldn't shake the feeling that there was something wrong. "Why only the one?"

Sarah pointed ahead. "There's more. There's one. And over there."

She carefully checked out several of the prints before turning back to Travis, a look of bafflement on her face.

"They're all lefts," she said. "Like there was only one foot involved."

Travis looked. Sure enough, all the prints were from a left boot; there was no mistaking it. But there was another mark as well, only quite different.

"What do you make of this?" Sarah asked.

Travis shook his head. "All these left prints and these marks like little trenches."

"Like whatever it was – or *whoever* it was," said Sarah, "was dragging something."

"Exactly," said Travis.

Both of them looked up at each other at the same time, both with their mouths open in astonishment.

"It couldn't be!" said Travis.

"B-b-but," stammered Sarah, "what *else* could it be?"

Travis could hardly believe he was mouthing the word.

"*Slewfoot?*"

16

TRAVIS AND SARAH WERE STILL TRYING TO FIND their tongues when they noticed they were no longer alone in the campsite. Rachel had come back so quietly they hadn't even noticed.

Only something was different about Rachel. She didn't have any water with her, though she was still carrying the empty plastic container. And she looked as if she'd just had the scare of her life.

"Get the others up," she said in a voice so quiet they barely heard her.

"Why?" Travis said. "What's wrong?"

"There's something you have to see in the swamp."

Travis and Sarah scrambled to wake the others up while Rachel stood off to the side of the camp, staring back in the direction of the swamp. She looked terrified.

"I got nothin' to wear!" Nish moaned when they finally spun him out of his sleeping bag.

He'd grown hot in the night and taken off everything but his infamous boxers. He'd stuffed his shorts and shirt into what he thought was a safe corner of the tent, but the rain had soaked right through where his clothes touched the sides and now they were as drenched as if they'd just come out of a washing machine.

"Offer still stands, Big Boy," Sam said, pulling a fresh sweatshirt out of her pack.

"I'm not wearing that crud!" Nish whined. "Anybody sees me, they'll think I'm in a Gay Pride Parade!"

"Suit yourself, Big Boy. We're off. The pack's right here if you need anything."

They set off with Rachel in the lead. She led them down the small creek path that ran from the side of the hill. It was still bubbling with last night's rainfall, and the going was tough at times. The rocks were slippery. The overgrowth was a tangle on both sides, the tag alders and aspen and cedar all but impenetrable, meaning they really had no choice but to continue down through the creek.

The terrain flattened out near the bottom, swamp on both sides and the creek winding through the bog towards a slightly larger creek, running clean and fast. This must have been where Rachel had come in search of drinking water.

There were bulrushes here, and tall blueberry

bushes everywhere. The ground was spongy, and every so often their feet sank right down into the bog. Dead tamarack trees stood, or had fallen, almost everywhere the kids looked.

Rachel was pointing at something through a narrow opening of cedar.

Travis could see nothing at first, but then he noticed the damaged trees, pine and cedar snapped off as if something had exploded through the swamp, the fresh wood bright and shining where the trunks and branches had broken.

The huge swath through the trees made an easy trail for the eye to follow.

And then he saw it, out in the middle of the swamp with large pools of water on all sides.

He saw the splash of red first. But then white, a structure looming large like a curved doorway. It had letters on it: YT . . .

It was the tail of an airplane!

17

IT SEEMED LIKE THE LONGEST TIME BEFORE anyone spoke.

"Jake Tyson's plane!" Travis gasped, finally.

"Has to be," said Rachel.

"Is–is–is there any sign of . . . life?" Fahd sputtered.

"I tried to get over," Rachel said. "I couldn't. So I came back for you guys."

"*We have to get to it!*" Sarah all but shrieked. She was shaking, almost crying.

"You'll sink if you try to walk to it," said Rachel. "I tried. We'll have to come at it from the far side, and with branches."

It took a while for the Owls to understand what Rachel meant. Before she led them back to this spot, she had picked up the tool she had used to build the shelter, and after the six kids had worked their way around to the far side of the swamp, she immediately went to work cutting and sawing saplings, leaving their branches and leaves intact.

"We can work a bridge over with these," she said.

It took them the better part of two hours, but slowly, ever so slowly, they worked their way closer to the sunken, smashed aircraft.

Rachel's idea was ingenious. She would lay down a sapling, sometimes two, on the surface of the bog, making a bridge between one fairly solid clump of grass and moss and the next. They kept a steady stream of fresh saplings and branches coming, and gradually formed a path over the bog.

"*Is it Jake?*"

The voice came from well behind. Nish had caught up with them.

They stood up from their work and stared back through the underbrush.

Nish had arrived in full sequinned glory! He had selected Sam's most discreet sweatshirt and shorts, but he still sparkled like a jewellery counter as he stood before them, his face like a glistening ruby.

"No cracks!" he ordered. "Is it Jake?"

"We don't know," said Sam, acting as if nothing at all were unusual about Nish's appearance.

"We haven't made it to the plane yet," said Rachel. "Can you do some cutting?"

Nish was anxious to help. He took the tool and began sawing off branches and handing them along as the others worked their way closer.

As they inched deeper into the bog, the heavier Owls dropped back. Nish was already well back. But Sam dropped off, then Sarah. The three smaller ones – Rachel, Fahd, and Travis – continued to build the bridge out until they were just a few feet from the craft.

Carefully, Rachel laid down the last of the branches. It stretched to within an arm's length of the fuselage of the plane.

Travis could clearly see the damage now. The wings had been sheared off as the plane cut down through the trees. The engine had been torn away from its housing and lay, smashed, half buried in the muck. The pontoons, from what little he could see of them, seemed *squashed* by the fuselage, which had pounded down onto them on impact.

"One of us has to check," Rachel said.

"I can't," Fahd said, near tears. "I just can't do it, okay?"

"I'll do it," said Travis.

He had no idea where the bravery had come from. He was Travis Lindsay, the kid who still liked to sleep with a night light on, the kid who was so terrified last night he couldn't even look out to see what was making that terrible noise. The idea of staring down into the cockpit at two dead men terrified him. What, he wondered, if they were still alive? No, they couldn't be. Impossible. But if they weren't alive, then they had to be dead. He couldn't do it. But he had to . . .

He had to because Rachel was here. Rachel, who had found the plane, who had made it possible for them to be dry and warm through the night, who was the best chance the Owls had of ever getting out of here.

And he was team captain.

"I'll go," he repeated.

He felt Rachel touch his arm. "Be careful," she whispered.

Travis took one tentative step onto the makeshift bridge. It held fine. He tightrope-walked his way along the branches and made the final lunge onto the crunched pontoon.

"*Don't cut yourself!*" Fahd cried out.

Travis looked back. He could see his friends staring at him as if he were about to do something incredible, like explode, or vanish into the muck.

No one seemed to be breathing. Nish appeared even to have forgotten he was wearing a pink sweatshirt with purple and silver sequins and bluejean cutoffs with copper studs sewn on to make a big heart right over his butt.

Travis surveyed the wreck. For a fleeting moment, he thought it might have been here for some time, that in fact it wasn't the plane in which Jake Tyson had been flying. But that made no sense; the plane might be a wreck, but the paint was new.

There were small foot- and hand-holds along the pilot's side of the plane, and one of the wing struts was still half on, a convenient step to get to the small door.

Travis reached out to pull himself up, then stepped onto the strut.

He took a deep breath. He had no choice. He had to look. There could be no turning back now.

"*Travis! Be careful!*" Rachel called out.

Travis nodded. He would not turn back. Something in Rachel's voice made him realize he would crawl through broken glass and land mines and writhing cobras, if necessary.

He pulled himself higher.

The window at the side had blown out on impact.

He eased himself up, his heart pounding so loud and fast he thought it must be shaking the entire plane.

He looked in.

The pilot was slumped over the controls. His head was bloody around the temples and ears, and his neck was twisted unnaturally.

He was staring straight at Travis.

Travis almost jumped back, but he knew he couldn't. If he dropped down onto the soft moss and bog, he would sink in to his armpits.

He forced himself to keep looking.

There was no question about it – the pilot was dead. He had probably been dead from the moment the plane struck, just like that other pilot who'd been flying Bill Barilko so many years ago. Both of them had died instantly, still sitting in their seats when the plane was finally found.

Travis made himself look beyond the pilot.

Seeing the dead face of a total stranger was bad enough, Travis thought. But he knew he would recognize Jake Tyson.

His stomach lurched. He was going to throw up. He forced it back down, the vomit burning in his throat, and he swallowed deliberately, stepped high again, and looked over the jumble of packs and fishing supplies that had been thrown forward when the plane crashed into the bog.

The passenger seat was empty!

The passenger door was swinging open and bent, almost as if it had been kicked open.

Wherever Jake Tyson was, he wasn't here!

18

TRAVIS HAD WITNESSED ENOUGH: THE SMELL OF death, the wildly buzzing flies, the pilot staring back at him through lifeless eyes.

He again felt like he was going to vomit. He shook his head to throw off the thought, and carefully stepped down.

"*What is it?*" Sam called.

Travis had almost forgotten that they were waiting for him. He tried to speak, but nothing came out. He could feel his throat tighten. "There's only one – and he's dead!" was all he could manage to say.

"*Is it Jake!*" Nish called, his voice breaking.

Travis shook his head, no.

"Check the radio," Rachel said.

Travis cringed, but he knew she was right. The radio might still be working, and if he could only turn it on, the rescue craft might pick up the signal.

He forced himself to step back up to the open window. Fighting to keep his eyes off the pilot, he reached until his shoulder was half in the window, flicked the radio switch, and realized it was already on. The radio was dead.

Of course. They'd been signalling just before the plane crashed – probably right up until the plane hit the swamp.

"No good – it's dead," Travis shouted as he stepped down.

"We have to look for Jake," said Fahd.

"Maybe he was thrown when it hit the trees," suggested Rachel

They searched throughout the swamp. They searched along the path the plane had cut through the trees, in case the passenger door had burst open and he'd been thrown out.

"He's just vanished!" said Sam.

"Maybe he sank," suggested Sarah.

"It's not deep enough anywhere," said Fahd.

They searched the immediate area again, but found nothing. No sign whatsoever of Jake Tyson, the hero of the Stanley Cup.

"*There's something over here!*" called Rachel.

It was a man's shirt, muddy and soaking wet. Rachel carefully spread it out on the ground. *The right arm was missing.*

"A one-armed man!" said Nish. "Just like in that movie – whatyacallit?"

"*The Fugitive*," Fahd said, without even thinking.

Rachel held up her hand for the boys to shut up. They did so immediately. "I'd guess he was having more trouble with one of his legs than his arm," she said. "I think he ripped the sleeve off to make a tourniquet."

"What's *that* mean?" said Nish.

"It means Jake Tyler's still alive."

No one said a word.

"Or," added Rachel, "at least he was when he stopped here to try to stop the bleeding."

She got up and headed back towards the plane, where the pilot still lay dead against the controls.

"*Be careful!*" Sarah shouted after her.

"*Give me a hand, Trav,*" Rachel called back.

Together, the two of them made their way out to the craft, carefully stepping along sapling branches to approach the wreck from the passenger side.

Rachel checked the bent and torn passenger door, still loosely hanging off one of its hinges, then she crawled onto the busted pontoon and leaned in the doorway at floor level and looked around.

She ducked back out, sucking in wind to catch her breath. When she looked at Travis, he noticed a large drop roll down her cheek and fall from her chin. He thought at first it was sweat, but when he looked into her eyes he knew that it had been a tear, with others now following.

"There's an awful lot of blood on the floor in here," she said matter-of-factly. "There's metal ripped up from the floor, too. He must have been cut badly. There's blood on the door at the bottom as well. Maybe he had to kick it out."

"*Track* him," Nish suggested after Travis and Rachel had come back.

Rachel looked up at him, smiled quickly, and shook her head. "That only works in the movies, silly. Maybe you'd like me to send smoke signals off to Muck and the rangers, too?"

Nish blushed deeply. "I didn't mean it like that," he sputtered.

"We *have* to look for him!" said Sam. "*We have to!*"

Rachel nodded, looking up at Travis. "She's right," she said. "We've got to stay here."

"How long?" Nish asked, a tremor in his voice.

"Until we find him," said Rachel.

"Or they find us."

19

"ARE YOU THINKING THE SAME THING I AM?" Sarah whispered when she and Travis were out of hearing range of the others.

"I don't know. What're you thinking?"

"It was Jake Tyson walking through our campsite last night, not Slewfoot."

Travis nodded, but he had no idea what to say next. Ever since Rachel had said the missing shirt sleeve might have been used as a tourniquet to stop the bleeding in Jake Tyson's leg, Travis had been wondering the same thing.

"Why wouldn't he wake us?" Travis asked.

"There's one possibility," said Sarah.

"Which is?"

"He's had a head injury. Maybe he doesn't know who he is. Maybe he has amnesia."

"But not remembering who you are doesn't mean you wouldn't get help if you could."

"I don't know – perhaps he's not thinking right, or he thinks we did it to him or something. It just seems to me that if Rachel's right and he's got a badly hurt leg he might be dragging, then that would explain the marks around the campsite this morning."

"I agree," said Travis. "I never believed that stupid story about Slewfoot anyway."

Sarah smiled gently at him. "No one ever believes those stories unless it's three o'clock in the morning."

Travis looked quickly at her, puzzled, then realized what she was saying. Stories like Slewfoot required an imagination to run away with them.

He smiled back. "You got that one right."

Sarah and Travis showed the others the markings in the ground when they returned to camp. Nish seemed extremely nervous, as if now not only did he have little green men to worry about *and* his favourite hockey hero, but mad Slewfoot was invading the camp at night.

"I-I-I don't really think we should stay here tonight," he said.

Sam clucked her tongue. "If Jake's around here, he needs us. He could be dying, for all we know."

"We're agreed we stay and look until we find him – or until the others find us?" said Sarah.

"We have to," said Fahd.

"There's no other option," said Sam.

"None," said Travis.

"We should get searching," said Rachel.

"*Can't I eat first?*" moaned Nish.

20

THEY SEARCHED FIRST FOR MORE SIGNS OF JAKE Tyson, but they had no further luck.

"Nothing," Travis said as he returned to the camp.

"Nothing here, either," said a disappointed Sam.

"Not a thing," said Fahd. "If he's out there, he's probably dead by now."

"*Don't say that!*" Sarah practically screamed. "He's here somewhere – and he's hurt!"

No one said anything for a while.

Nish came walking up the trail with the front of Sam's pink sweatshirt held out in front of him like a tray. From the look on his face, he seemed terribly proud of himself.

"I found us some blueberries," he announced.

Holding the sweatshirt with one hand, he reached for a handful with the other – just as Rachel lunged and struck the pouch of the shirt from below with her fist, sending the berries flying.

"*What the –?*" said a startled Nish.

Rachel was already prying open Nish's chubby

clenched fist of berries, knocking the squashed black fruit to the ground.

"*Are you nuts?*" Nish shouted.

"*These aren't blueberries!*" Rachel shouted back. "*They're deadly nightshade – poisonous!*"

"Whadyamean?"

Rachel leaned down and picked up one of the berries. "Look at it," she said. "It's black, not blue, and about three times the size of a blueberry."

"*Big* blueberries," Nish argued feebly. "And very sweet."

Rachel looked with horror at Nish, who was scarlet.

"You *didn't* eat any, did you?"

"Not these ones – but before, on that portage . . ."

"What portage?" said Sam.

"That first one, where we all ate blueberries. I found this big bush with huge berries on it. But there were only a couple I could reach."

"Blueberries grow on little bushes," Sarah said.

"You *ate* two?" Rachel asked.

Nish nodded, growing ever redder.

"Well, then, that explains it, doesn't it?"

Nish was flabbergasted. "Explains *what*?"

"Your flying saucer. . . . It's a wonder you weren't sick to your stomach, too."

Nish blinked. "Well, if you must know, I was. I went outside to throw up, that's how come I was there when they tried to abduct me."

Rachel shook her head, grinning. "You have to be the luckiest jerk in the world, Nish. If you'd eaten more, you'd probably be dead. Witches used to use it to make people think they were flying. But it can kill you if you eat too much."

Nish looked down at his berry-stained hands. He tried to wipe them off.

"Go to the creek and wash up," Rachel told him. "We'll start up a fire. And stay away from black berries, okay?"

"And watch out for space aliens while you're at it!" giggled Sam.

Nish wandered off to clean up and the rest busied themselves collecting wood and starting the fire. Rachel built the fire but kept sending the Owls back into the brush for more wood and kindling.

"Why so much wood?" Sarah asked.

"We'll keep a good fire burning all night," Rachel said. "We couldn't in the storm, but if we do tonight he might see it or smell it. It might bring him around again."

"And if that happens?" asked Sam.

Rachel shrugged. "Maybe this time he'll ask for help. Maybe last night he was disoriented."

They decided to sleep in shifts, making sure there were two awake at all times to feed the fire. Fahd programmed his wristwatch to go off every two hours so they could switch.

Nish and Travis drew the two o'clock to four

o'clock shift. The fire was still going strong when they took over from Sam and Sarah, and Travis built it up even higher by throwing on several more logs.

It was a beautiful night, the sky so clear the stars seemed close enough to touch. The fire snapped and crackled and periodically hissed as a wet piece of wood fizzled and steamed and eventually began to burn. It was too warm to sit close, and the boys backed off, leaning against trees as they watched the fire dance shadows around the camp and over the little tent where Fahd was now sleeping alone.

They tried to name the constellations, but Travis could only handle Orion and the Big and Little Dipper before he gave up and just stared into the starry depths of the Milky Way.

It was August – the time, the rangers had said, of the meteor showers – and they watched in amazement as falling stars spurted across the sky and then disappeared. They counted up to thirty, several times seeing two or more at once, before Travis heard a familiar sound beside him.

Nish snoring.

He had dozed off in the warm darkness. His head was lolling on his chest. Travis knew it was unfair – the whole idea of taking a watch together was to keep each other awake – but he didn't really care. Anyway, if he shook him awake, Nish would just fall right back to sleep.

Besides, Travis didn't really want to talk. He wanted to think. He wanted to go over this incredible adventure and try to make sense of it. He'd been so excited to go off on this trip with the Owls, so pleased to learn that Jesse would be bringing along his cousin, Rachel. And it had all begun so perfectly.

Right up until Nish saw his stupid spaceship.

Now they were lost in the deep woods. They were lost without proper equipment or food, with no sign that they'd be found any time soon. And a short distance away a man lay dead against the controls of a crashed airplane, his passenger nowhere to be found.

●

Travis didn't remember feeling sleepy, but he must have nodded off. When he opened his eyes he was still leaning against the tree, and he was staring straight into the eyes of the wolf.

The wolf was sitting off to the side of the fire, staring back.

Travis hadn't heard a thing. He had simply felt, once again, that strange *tickle* of someone's eyes on him.

The wolf looked fierce, terrifying – but also unbelievably beautiful. His coat was thick and dark and seemed almost to shine in the light of the fire. But most remarkable were the eyes. Travis had never seen eyes like this before in his life. They were yellow, like beams. Other times they looked red, like the fire. And always they seemed to pass right through and into him, like lasers.

He felt afraid, and then he felt not at all afraid. It was the strangest of feelings.

The wolf could easily kill him. It was huge. It could bring down a full-grown moose with its powerful jaws. And yet Travis felt no need to worry that anything was about to happen to him or the others. Not even to chubby Nish, snoring and burbling and grunting like a pig at the foot of the other tree.

The wolf stared for several seconds, raised itself from its haunches and sauntered off to the far side of the camp.

It turned, looked once back over its shoulder, and disappeared into the woods.

Travis watched after it for the longest time, but he could see no movement at all under the pitch-black branches of the spruce trees.

He thought he had fallen asleep again. Something had shifted.

The light.

He was bathed in moonlight. The moon had risen over the treetops now and was shining down into the little glade where they had made camp. It was bright enough to read by.

Travis looked up at the sky again. It was as if the moon had taken all its brightness from the stars. He could see some, particularly low in the sky, but nothing around the moon, which seemed to have gained a halo of light. There were no more meteors.

The first howl felt like someone had stuck an ice-cold fish knife straight into his spine.

"AWWWWOOOOOOOOOHHHHHHHHHHH!"

"*W-w-w-wazzat?*"

The voice belonged to Nish. He was terrified.

"I think it's a wolf," said Travis.

"*A wolf? Where?*"

"He was here a minute ago – right by the fire."

"WHAT?" Nish scrambled to his feet,

"AWWWWOOOOOOO–OOOOOOHHHHHHHHH!"

The howl came from the far end of the campsite.

Nish jumped up and reached for a stick, brandishing it as he backed off.

"WOLVES KILL PEOPLE!" Nish shouted.

There was movement in the lean-to. Rachel's head appeared, followed by Sam's, her eyes still blinking with sleep.

"What's happening?" Rachel asked.

"There was a wolf here. That's it howling."

"AWW–WWW–WWWOOO–OOOHHH–HHH!"

"He's just howling at the moon," said Rachel.

"That's the most frightening sound I've ever heard," said Sam.

Sarah was up now, too, and a moment later the

zipper sounded in the little tent and Fahd's sleepy head poked out.

"What's that awful sound?" Fahd asked.

"A wolf," Travis said. He was surprised at his own calmness. It was almost as if he *knew* the wolf, and knew instinctively that everything would be all right.

"I'M GETTIN' OUTTA HERE!" Nish shouted, reaching now for the axe-shovel, which he held up like he was carrying a machine gun.

"*You can't go anywhere!*" Sam screamed at him. "*You'll get lost!*"

"*What the heck's wrong with you?*" Nish shouted back at her. "*We're already lost!!!*"

And with that he turned and ran straight back into the woods, directly away from the sounds of the howling wolf.

"AWWWWOOOOOOOOHHHHHHHHHH!"

Travis hurried to his feet. Sam and Rachel were already out, ready to give chase.

All they could hear was Nish crashing through the bush, branches snapping, Nish grunting as he bounced from tree to tree.

And then they heard a sound that made the wolf's howl seem like a lullaby.

"AAAAAEEEEEEEEEEEEEEEEEEEEEEEEEEEEEE!!!!!!!"

It was Nish, screaming.

Screaming as if the world had come to an end.

21

NISH WAS SOBBING, HIS CHEST HEAVING SO FAST
it seemed, at first, as if he might be laughing.

He had tripped over something and fallen hard
into it.

Fahd's flashlight swept over whatever had
dumped Nish.

It was no rock, no tree, certainly no wolf.

It was Jake Tyson.

●

The sky was lightening by the time they hauled
the injured hockey player back into the camp. He
was out cold, but alive. His body was convulsing
horribly, and sometimes it seemed as if he were
about to jump right out of his own skin.

They got Jake Tyson settled by the fire and
covered him with sleeping bags, but still he
shook.

Sarah, who had taken a first-aid course, began
taking charge. She checked his breathing and his
eyes and pulse, then sent Rachel for the water
container. They soaked one of Sam's shirts, and

Sarah put the damp edge of it into Tyson's mouth. He was still out, but his lips automatically began sucking at the moisture.

Fahd and Sarah checked Tyson's injured leg. They'd been right: he was wearing a tourniquet made from the sleeve of a shirt. Sarah loosened it and, after a while, tied it again when it became clear the blood was still flowing out of the ugly gash on the back of his calf. He was wearing hiking shorts, and the bare leg was covered in blood; Sarah very carefully washed as much off as she could. She checked his eyes again. They looked milky, lost. But his breathing was strong, if rapid.

"He's lost a lot of blood," Sarah said after a while. "We have to get him out of here."

"And how do we do that?" said Nish with unnecessary sarcasm.

"We have to get help," she said. "If we don't get help soon, it's going to be bad."

"How bad?" asked Fahd, who always asked the questions no one else would.

Sarah didn't answer. There were tears in her eyes.

"What do we do?" Travis asked.

"Someone's going to have to hike out," she said. "If they can't find us, we're going to have to get someplace where we can find them."

"I'll go," said Travis, suddenly brave.

"And me," said Rachel.

Sarah shook her head. "Rachel has to stay. We'll need water and food for him if he comes around, and she's the best at that."

"I'll help," said Sam.

"I'll take care of the fire," said Fahd.

Sarah looked up at Travis and Nish. "That leaves you two," she said. "Do you think you can do it?"

"We don't know *what* to do!" said an exasperated Nish.

"Take the orange tarp," said Rachel. "It's big and it's bright, and if they can't see that, they can't see anything."

"But where do we go?" asked Travis, beginning to get unnerved.

"Follow the little creek to the big one," said Rachel. "Water always flows to more water. It's in an easterly direction. My guess is it will take you out to the Crow River, eventually. If you don't find Muck, there will be other trippers going through."

"And if not," added Sarah, "you'd need to find a high point of land – a bluff, maybe – where you could put out the tarp so one of the planes might see it."

"We'll keep a smoky fire going here," said Fahd. "And we'll be west of where they pick you up."

"Good point, Fahd," said Sarah. "If they find you two, they'll find us."

"What if they find you before they find us?" Nish suddenly wailed.

"I intend to say you were never with us," said Sam, her joke relieving some of the tension.

"*You would!*" snarled Nish. "C'mon, Trav, let's save everybody! Just like we always have to!"

22

THE GOING WAS ROUGH. THEY HAD A PACK holding the large orange tarpaulin, some berries and a change of clothes for each – Nish still having to live with Sam's sequin madness – and they had only the vaguest idea of where they were heading.

Nish seemed to have forgotten entirely that he was dressed so oddly. Travis no longer even considered it funny. They were tired, but they were also determined to get where they needed to be.

They followed the creek. At times it was barely a trickle, at others the flow was so strong it seemed it would be only a turn or two before they came out onto a river. But whenever they got their hopes up, the flow returned to a trickle.

Several times they headed down false leads, only to have to come back to where the creek had split and try again.

The growth along the sides of the ever-widening creek was dense and thick and difficult. There were hawthorns, with sharp stabbing pricks, scratching raspberry bushes, and thistles. Travis and Nish were hot and sticky and the bugs were terrible.

Nish hardly said a word. Normally, Travis thought, his friend would be moaning and complaining at every setback, but not this time. Nish ground ahead with that look of determination Travis knew so well from important hockey games, when all of a sudden, much to everyone's surprise, Nish would quit playing the fool and become the hardest-working member of the team and the very best teammate in the world.

Nish pushed on, his chubby butt making the copper-stud heart on the back of his borrowed cutoffs wiggle from side to side, but Travis couldn't even bring himself to smile. He was proud of Nish, and glad to follow him.

They paused for a break, the boys cupping cold water in their hands and letting it run down the backs of their necks. They opened the pack and ate some berries, careful to keep a good portion for later, when they would need it more.

Travis lay down on an open spot along the bank, closing his eyes. When he opened them, he thought he was having a vision.

He could see something in the distance that seemed to rise twice as high as the highest pines.

"What's that?" Travis asked.

"Some kind of tower, I guess."

Travis sat up fast. "It's a *fire* tower."

"A *what*?"

"A fire tower — they were marked on the big map when we started out, remember?"

"No."

"They were built all through the park to watch for fires in the old days. But they do it all by airplane now. Some of the towers are still standing, though — they're tourist attractions for the canoe trippers."

"Big deal," said Nish.

"It *is* a big deal. If we can climb up and unfurl the tarp like a flag, a plane is sure to see it."

"I'm not climbing nothing," said Nish. "I don't like heights, remember?"

"I'll do it," Travis said. "I don't mind."

They made for the fire tower. Occasionally it was lost from view, but then a break would come in the tree cover and they'd see it again, looming above a nearing hill. Travis was astonished at how high it was.

"You wouldn't catch me going up something like that for all the money in the world," said Nish.

They arrived at a dried creek bed that came down from the hill and now were able to make good time. Travis was so excited he began to run, jumping from rock to rock. He could see this working, could see the planes spotting their sign.

He even saw Jake Tyler being rescued in time. He was no longer scared. He was happy, full of hope.

And then he fell.

●

"This is just not happening to me!"

"There's no other way," Travis said. His sandal had skidded on a rock he'd been leaping to, and his ankle had twisted. Badly.

He thought at first it was broken; the pain was so intense he cried. He was not ashamed to cry. It hurt that much.

He tried to put some weight on it and decided it wasn't broken, but it was probably sprained. He could only hobble. He couldn't continue up the creek bed very quickly, and he certainly couldn't climb the fire tower.

"You *have* to," he said to Nish.

"I *can't*. You know that!"

Travis did know. Nish was petrified of heights.

"There's no other way," Travis said again.

"I *can't*," Nish repeated. He was openly bawling now.

"It's not for me," said Travis. "It's for Jake."

Nish said nothing. He was clutching the edge of the tarp and staring up at the fire tower. He was shaking. Travis played the last card he held. "Jake will die, Nish . . . he'll die if you don't give him a chance."

Nish's sequin-covered chest was heaving now he was crying so hard. Tears were pouring out of him and his cheeks were tomato-red. Travis didn't think he had ever seen his friend in such bad shape.

"Jake will die," he repeated.

Nish didn't say a word. He picked up the tarp, stuffed it into his own pack, pulled the pack on, shifted it around, and turned to climb up the fire tower.

23

NISH TRIED TO CONVINCE HIMSELF HE WAS JUST climbing some stairs. He told himself he was going to bed, that he was walking up to the science lab at Lord Stanley Public School, that he was simply heading up into the stands at the Tamarack rink.

But it was no use. He knew exactly where he was. There was a sign posted at the bottom of the fire tower: *Keep Off! Extreme Danger. Trespassers Will Be Prosecuted*.

Nish found the sign amusing, at least. If only the police were here to arrest him, then he wouldn't have to do it. If only there were video cameras watching the fire tower, he would just have to stand in front of it and wave.

The wooden steps were rickety and rotten. Some were broken. Nish adjusted his pack and began climbing, his eyes shut tight, refusing, at all costs, to look down. The only metal in the entire structure would be the nails, and he wasn't sure about them. The wood had rotted away around many of them. Others were missing.

"I'm gonna die," he said out loud. "Simple as that – I am going to die!"

He worked his way up slowly. He tried to think of nothing but the climb: *first one hand, then the other, one step at a time, stop and rest whenever necessary, don't forget to breathe, NEVER LOOK DOWN, NO MATTER WHAT.*

He kept count as he climbed. It seemed to calm his mind. He counted out loud.

". . . Forty-one . . . forty-two . . . forty-three . . .

". . . Seventy-six . . . seventy-seven . . . seventy-eight . . ."

He would soon reach a hundred. He could feel the wind up here. He could feel – he was sure! – the structure swaying in the wind. He wondered if he was the only person in history who had ever climbed a fire tower with his eyes shut.

Hand over hand, foot over foot – up, up, up he climbed.

The wind was sharper now, buffeting him and forcing him to stop more often to gather his breath.

". . . Ninety-one . . . ninety-two . . . ninety-three . . .

". . . One hundred and twelve . . . one hundred and thirteen . . . one hundred and fourteen . . ."

His head hit something.

Nish opened his eyes. He could see forever. It was as if he were flying. He could see white pines reaching up far, far above the rest of the forest, but none of them nearly as high as him. He could see distant hills, blue in the haze. He could see clouds.

He had reached the cabin at the top of the tower. It had seemed so small from the ground, but now that he was at the top, he was surprised at how large it was. Like a small cottage in the sky.

He hurried up through an open trap door and onto the platform surrounding the lookout cabin. He dared not look down.

"I'm going to pass out," he said to himself. "I'm going to fall down right here and never get up again. I'm going to curl up into a ball and cry until someone climbs up and saves me . . ."

But there was no one to save him. No one at all.

He muscled off his pack, pulled out the orange tarp, and carefully unfolded it. The wind was gusting hard up here. It snapped at the corners of the tarp, the sound like gunfire as Nish tried to open it up. He'd have to tie it down.

There were plastic ties already on the tarp. He tied as many as he could to a small flagpole on the platform, and when he thought it was solid enough, he let it go.

The tarp roared out into the wind, snapping viciously off the end of the platform.

Nish ducked back down, leaning hard against the little cabin. *The cabin!* He thought. I can get in out of the wind.

He reached up, still on his knees, and tried the door. It gave.

The cabin was a mess: old pots and pans, mouse nests, faded newspapers and curled and torn magazines, a single chair, a small table, some built-in cupboards. The names of previous visitors had been scribbled or carved everywhere. Most people had added dates, and they shocked him – 1947, 1938, 1952, 1961 – all long before he was even born.

How long would it be, he wondered, before this whole thing toppled in the wind?

He was too tired to care. He lay on the floor, staring up out of the window, and tried to shut out the screaming of the wind and the violent snapping of the tarp.

Nish must have fallen asleep. He had no idea how long he had been lying there. It might have been hours. It might have been only a few minutes. But suddenly he was wide awake. The snapping had *stopped*.

Nish got unsteadily to his feet and forced himself to the window, staring out at the pole.

The tarp was gone! It must have just happened, because when he looked out he could see it flying like a leaf through the air, swinging one way then the other as it fell. It must have been the sudden silence that had woken him. *He hadn't tied it tightly enough!*

Nish fell to his knees, sobbing. He had failed everyone. He had killed Jake Tyson.

And then he heard another sound, distant at first, like a low growl. He crawled back to the window, got to his knees, and looked out, scanning the hills.

The tarp was still in the air, but beyond it there was something yellow.

One of the rangers' Otters – a search-and-rescue plane.

It banked sharply to avoid the flying orange tarp then turned again towards the fire tower.

Nish suddenly found himself on his feet. He was pulling open the door and jumping out onto the platform, waving madly and screaming. "HERE! HERE! HERE! SAVE ME! SAVE ME! SAVE ME!"

The yellow Otter was coming straight for him, then banked away.

"NOOOOOO!" Nish screamed. "I'M HERE! IT'S ME – NISH!!!"

The plane banked again, then tipped its wings twice at him. The plane turned sharply right in front of Nish and he could see the pilot. He was giving Nish the thumbs-up.

He'd been seen!

"I'M A HERO!!" Nish screamed into the howling wind.

And then he looked below.

He still had to get down.

24

TRAVIS WAS AWARE OF NOTHING BUT THE TWO slim arms around him.

He thought he was going to burst.

He thought he was going to die – absolutely happy.

The hug was from Rachel. It had followed the hug from Sam, which had followed the hug from Sarah – and somewhere in there had been a back-slap from Fahd – but this one was different. Travis was certain his feelings would be written all over his face when she finally let go of him.

If she ever let go . . .

The Screech Owls were back together. The Natural Resources yellow rescue helicopter had touched down by the fire tower, and Travis, with his ankle swelled up like a balloon, had been waiting at the foot of the wooden steps when the two rangers ducked under the slowing blades of the big chopper and came running towards him.

At first they thought he was alone. They figured he had twisted his ankle coming down the ladder.

That's when Travis told the rangers there were two of them – that Nish was still somewhere up above. Travis hadn't heard a word from his pal since he'd seen the big orange plastic tarp go sailing off into the wind just before the search-and-rescue plane made its wide turn and tipped its wings twice to signal they'd been seen.

The rangers had to climb the tower and lead Nish down as if he were blind and helpless. One came down just ahead of him, carefully placing Nish's feet on each step, while the other followed close behind, a rope tied from his shoulders around Nish's thick waist.

Nish climbed down with his eyes closed.

Travis couldn't help but giggle. The rangers must have wondered about Nish's sequinned sweatshirt and cutoffs with the copper-stud heart on the butt.

If they thought it odd – and surely they did – they were too polite to poke fun at him. They got Nish down and helped him lie on the ground, and Travis knew at once that the old Nish was back.

"My energy's down," he heard Nish whine to the rangers. "You didn't bring any chocolate bars, did you?"

The helicopter dropped them back at their old campsite on Big Crow Lake. The others had already been rescued – Fahd, Sam, Sarah, and

Rachel none the worse for wear – and the rest of the Screech Owls had been flown in from the river near Lake Laveille, Muck's treasured fishing lake.

The two older rangers, Tom McCormick and Jerry Kennedy, were still at the campsite, and the two younger rangers, Dick Chancey and André Girard, had just come back from helping airlift Jake Tyson out. Medics aboard the chopper had whisked the injured hockey star out to Tamarack, where he was put on an air ambulance that flew him straight to hospital down south.

"He'll live," André told the group. "He may never play hockey again, but he'll live."

Travis was certain he saw Muck flinch. Muck would be thinking about how his own leg got smashed so many years ago and what it had done to his NHL dreams.

"Why didn't he ask us for help?" Sam said.

André shrugged.

"He came to when we were airlifting him out," Dick said. "He seemed terrified of us. I don't think he knew *who* he was or *where* he was or who we were. He had a tremendous bump on his forehead."

"Amnesia is a funny thing," said the older ranger, Mr. Kennedy. "You never know how people will act or when they'll snap out of it."

Travis tried to imagine what it would be like not to remember anything of his past. Not his family, his grandparents, all the hockey and lacrosse teams he'd played on, the Screech Owls, Muck, Mr. Dillinger, all the tournaments they'd played in and all the fabulous places they'd visited . . .

Or Rachel.

No, he decided. It wouldn't matter how hard he hit his head – he'd never forget Rachel.

25

LIFE HAD RETURNED TO NORMAL.

The Owls were back home in Tamarack. The newspapers were reporting that Jake Tyson, the rookie hero of the previous spring's Stanley Cup final, had recovered his memory and was in rehabilitation for his damaged leg. He was sure he'd be back on the ice by Christmas. The first week of school was over and Nish had already raised his hand in science class and asked Mr. Schultz if there was any scientific proof that fish farted under water.

Best of all, the ice was back in at the Tamarack Memorial Arena and the Owls were getting ready for the new season.

Travis had walked down to the rink early on Saturday morning, just to take in the familiar sights and sounds and smells of his favourite place on earth. The rink had been freshly flooded, the new ice gleaming like a white sheet of paper waiting for Travis and the Owls to begin writing out the story of their new season. Mr. Dillinger was at his regular spot at the far end of the dressing room, his skate-sharpening machine open and running, a long arc of red and orange sparks flying off the end of one of Sarah's skate blades.

One by one, the Owls came in for the first practice, Nish dumping his hockey equipment down like it had spent the summer at the bottom of one of the town sewers, Sam and Sarah setting up beside each other on one side, Travis on the other, where he could have the best view of the entire room. They were all there – Fahd, Lars, Dmitri, Jeremy, Jenny with a new set of pads, Gordie grumbling that his skates were too small, Simon claiming he'd grown a full inch over the summer . . . even Data was already set up, his laptop computer glowing with the promise of a new breakout pattern for the team.

Travis felt right. He felt like he fit. He felt like life could not be much better.

Carefully he dressed, remembering the old, familiar, happy routine: jock, garter belt, left shinpad, right shinpad, socks, pants, skates, but not laced, shoulder pads, elbow pads . . .

"New sweaters this year!" Mr. Dillinger announced as he pushed in through the dressing-room door with a pile of white hockey jerseys over his back.

"*All right!*" cried out Andy.

"*Yes!*" shouted Sam.

Smiling to himself, Mr. Dillinger went around the room, hanging the new jerseys from the lockers of the dressing players.

Travis checked his anxiously and was relieved the "C" was still over the heart. He looked over at Sarah and Nish. They both had their "A"s, for alternate captain. And Sam had one too.

Sarah and Sam gave each other a thumb's-up. Nish, as usual, was scrambling to dress. He'd goofed around until everyone else was ready to head out and he hadn't even put on his skates.

Travis tied his skates, reached back, pulled down the new sweater, and inhaled its newness and cleanness as he pulled it quickly over his head, kissing the inside as always. Then he put on his neck guard and his helmet, picked up his gloves, and was ready to go.

Nish was racing. Not even he wanted to take the chance of upsetting Muck at the first practice of the new season. He was tying his skates so fast his fingers were a blur. He reached up, without looking, and yanked the new jersey off its hanger and pulled it over his head. He hopped up, pulled on his helmet and gloves, and, grabbing a stick, headed for the door.

He never even noticed that Mr. Dillinger had replaced his usual number 44 with sequins. All lovingly sewn on in the shape of a heart.

THE END

Murder at the Winter Games

The Screech Owls have gone to Salt Lake City for the Peewee Winter Games – with the championship game to be played on the same ice surface where the Canadian men and women hockey teams won Olympic Gold!

Nish has plans to run his own competition: the Gross-Out Olympics, featuring everything from taping players to dressing-room walls with duct tape to the "Snot Shot" – where players see how far they can fire a jellybean using only their noses. He also has a team contest to see who can figure out the Great Nish Secret and guess what the nuttiest Screech Owl of all has buried at centre ice for good luck.

But that secret pales once the Owls find out something strange – something terrifying – is going on in the tunnels beneath the magnificent hills surrounding the Olympic site.

Murder at the Winter Games *will be published by McClelland & Stewart in the fall of 2003.*

THE SCREECH OWLS SERIES